TO COVENTRY

A HUMMINGBIRD MURDER MYSTERY

T C PARKER

NEFARIOUS BAT PRESS

For Pin.
It's not Pillow Talk, but it's the best I can do.

CONTENT WARNINGS

While this novella is in many ways a dark comedy, it touches nevertheless on some very serious themes and topics about which I care deeply – and about which I, like many of the characters in the story, am pretty angry a lot of the time.

It's important, I think, not to shy away from discussion of these themes and topics, in fiction and elsewhere – but I have no interest in causing any reader undue distress.

Content warnings therefore apply for:

- Sexual assault (primarily off-page)
- Domestic violence (off-page and implied)
- Voyeurism (off-page)
- Revenge porn and digital sexual exploitation
- Misogyny
- Stalking / harassment (primarily implied)
- Murder / violence
- Blood / gore

Please do let me know via email if there are any others I should have included.

BEFORE

STU

The nosebleed came on as he was leaving the car park - a thin trickle of bright-red, copper-tasting mucus that coagulated into a clown's moustache on his upper lip. Must've been the weather, Stu told himself: the dry heat, irritating his nostrils. He should've drunk more water, moisturised more thoroughly; should've kept from picking his nose in the lift.

Or maybe it was the excitement that had brought it on. He'd been buzzing with it since he'd seen her, near-on vibrating with the urge to tell someone, *anyone*, what he'd witnessed. He should've taken a picture, he knew that; should've snatched an image – or better yet, a video of her, with his phone, before she slipped off into the crowd. Something to show to Matt and Ritesh when he met them later. Something to prove to himself that it really *had* happened, that she'd really *done* that - and, weirder still, that nobody around her had seemed to notice, or seemed to treat it as anything out of the ordinary.

He'd been too shocked to know *what* to do, at first. Then the migraine had started, the familiar pressure building behind his temples, throwing him off kilter. And before he could do the sensible thing and record what he was seeing, in spite of the pain, she'd just... vanished.

Which, now he thought about it, was pretty weird in itself, wasn't it?

At the roundabout, opposite the church where his cousin Alfie had got married the year before, the nosebleed intensified: thick, meaty blood gushing down his mouth and chin as fast as water from a tap, soaking his t-shirt. He pulled over as soon as he was able; stuck on his hazard lights, took a sports sock from his gym bag, and pressed it to his face to try to stem the flow.

He didn't panic, not immediately. Not until he glanced up at his reflection in the mirror to survey the damage and realised that his eyes, too, had begun to bleed.

He heard as well as felt it when his eardrums burst: a liquid bang inside his head, like wet corn popping in a microwave, accompanying a sensation of unseen fluids shifting course and a sudden change in the pressure around him, as if a hidden hand had thrust him underwater.

The windscreen and the world beyond it blurred, the fresh blood in his eyes throwing a red veil over his vision, and he fell forward, his forehead setting the car's horn blaring like a klaxon as it connected with the steering wheel.

More blood poured from his mouth. Before he knew what was happening, he was choking on it.

CHAPTER 1
SUNNY

Sunny isn't baking. Nor, she thinks, will she ever need to bake, in this brave new world of supermarket patisseries and kanafeh, as good as any she'd tasted in Constantinople, brought straight to one's door by polite young couriers on pedal-bikes.

She has, however, been unusually inclined to *watch* the baking of cakes and sweet pastries, these last days. Primarily by means of the tablet computer that rests currently on her outstretched legs - themselves resting on an Edwardian fainting couch which, though antique, is nonetheless younger by far than she is.

The tablet is newer: a gift, bestowed upon her by the significant other of a young man who may be the closest thing Sunny has currently to a friend. The young man, Jonas, has proven a positive influence on her mood, since the fates - not to say the machinations of a 17th century preacher hellbent on a transnational expurgation of sin - conspired to throw them together the previous summer. A cheerful, even-tempered counterbalance to the malaise with which she's been intermittently afflicted since the death, also the previous summer, of her *last* almost-friend.

Jonas' fiancé, Dan, is a software engineer by day, and an indefatigable *early adopter* in his leisure time – possessed of an enthusiasm for technology that would put the most ardent Canaanite to shame. For him, the tablet represents for Sunny nothing less than a panacea: a distraction from her grief, and a salve for her despondence.

"It'll help," he'd told her, just before he'd pressed the tiny slab of screen and hidden wire into her hands. "Give you something to entertain you while you're, you know... keeping yourself indoors."

He'd beamed at her, the very picture of obliging kindness, and she – reminding herself of Jonas, to whom she'd grown unexpectedly attached and who appeared, for his own reasons, to care deeply for the idiot boy before her – had accepted the offering. Neglecting, in a reciprocal act of kindness, to draw his attention to the shelves of books, the 90-inch television and the bone flutes that furnished the sitting room of her townhouse.

Both Jonas and Dan have visited her regularly since she decamped to the city from the countryside that was her home – electing to install herself in a Bloomsbury property she's kept, but neglected to visit with any real frequency, since the Belle Époque. In this moment, however, neither Dan nor Jonas is to be found within a thousand miles of Southampton Row. Instead, they are sunning themselves on the beaches of Miami, in celebration of their recent engagement, while Sunny, alone and uncharacteristically melancholy, lies like Bertha Pappenheim on her fainting couch, flicking languidly through reel upon reel of batters folded, sourdoughs kneaded and cupcakes frosted by hands unseen, their recipes incanted just off-screen by hidden pastry-cooks and self-described *cake artists*.

The rhythms of the videos are spellbinding, and though it pains her to admit it, she finds herself bewitched – even, as Dan had promised, *soothed*, her new-found sorrow quietened by the digitised pulses, their patterns and their flows.

She's scarcely a quarter of the way into the construction of a piña colada blondie when she's roused from torpor by the chiming of the doorbell: a synthesiser mangling of Liszt's Mephisto Polka Jonas had found utterly *hilarious* when he'd programmed the contraption. She knows, immediately and instinctively, which visitor she's apt to find waiting just beyond the door: not because she's received exactly one other guest than the boys since London called her, nor because the demonic acuity of her senses affords her a certain heightened insight one might easily mistake for prescience, but because the rattling of imitation-silver jewellery on the wrists and knuckles of her visitor would, even in the absence of this acuity, be thunderous enough to wake the dead.

"Could you *please* refrain from pressing that again?" she cries, not entirely hopeful that the intruder will hear her through the layers of brick and wood and plaster that stand between them, and much less so that she will show the necessary restraint; the intruder's ageing ears, after all, are nothing like so well-developed as Sunny's. And lo: not thirty seconds later, the Mephisto Polka plays again, tinny and unrelenting, stamping to dust the green shoots of Sunny's even temper.

She never cared for Liszt; had found him pompous and affected, even while the rest of Europe had succumbed to Lisztomania.

Thoroughly aggrieved, she rises from the couch, one hand cradling the tablet to her like a child's stuffed toy. Rises, and changes: the electric blue of her skin darkening to brown as the caprine joints of her lower legs straighten and reform and the hooves below them turn to five-toed feet. Her antlers, three feet high from base to tip, retract into her forehead with a brief, elastic snap. And suddenly she's human, or at the very least appears so: an adult woman, twenty-five or thirty, with no more and no less than the standard human complement of eyes and fingers.

Her visitor, she suspects, will appreciate the gesture; will be put at ease by Sunny's efforts at assimilation. More so still, perhaps, by the towelling dressing gown she retrieves from the bathroom on her way to the front door, and uses thereafter to conceal what her old, dead friend Miranda might have wryly termed her *modesty*.

"Jonas sent you, didn't he?" she says, as she flings the door open with what even *she* must concede is a melodramatic flourish.

"Did I get you out of bed?" The woman on the doorstep looks Sunny up and down, the pentacle necklace at her throat and the long grey plait she wears across one shoulder swaying discordantly with the dip and rise of her chin. She's dressed, as always, in the kind of flowing, wide-sleeved peasant dress Sunny once believed, erroneously, to have perished with the advent of the Industrial Revolution; a floppy felt hat better suited to a Hollywood warlock than a sixty-year-old English woman is perched atop her head. Her implicit critique of Sunny's present sartorial choices, therefore, cuts surprisingly deep.

Aggrieved, Sunny ignores the question, returning instead to her original line of attack. "Jonas. Your stepson.

Fruit of your husband's fecund loins. I assume *he* asked you to... how would he put it? *Check in* on me?"

"Not at all." For someone who purports to be a witch, albeit of a very different and altogether more benign bent than the hags and crones and daughters of the night with whom Sunny is more accustomed to dealing, the woman has no talent for duplicity. Crimson blotches, vivid as finger-prints, materialise on her cheeks and spread like ivy to her collarbone. When she speaks again, she's looking not at Sunny but at the toecaps of her own rainbow-coloured boots. "I was in the area. Wanted to pop in, see how you were."

"You lie appallingly, Fiona. Have the sisters of digital darkness never thought to mention this before?"

Fiona winces at the slight. It's a sore point for her, Sunny believes, that her de facto coven – a loose conglomeration of magically inclined women of a certain age, scattered about the globe – conduct their business principally by means of portable electrical devices not so very unlike Sunny's *tablet*: exchanging gossip, information and what wisdom they have to impart over instant messenger services, and coordinating biweekly sabbats via video conferencing services. The woman would clamber barefoot over broken glass for a bubbling cauldron on a windswept hilltop and a chance of going skyclad in the rain; of this, Sunny is certain.

"Are you going to invite me in?" Fiona says eventually. "It's bloody freezing out here, and not everybody's blessed with your...," she throws a second glance at the dressing gown, "... constitution."

"I'm busy," Sunny tells her, and closes the door.

It doesn't shut. Fiona, apparently anticipating such an outcome, has wedged a boot against the frame.

Not for the first time, Sunny curses the day Jonas – in

flagrant defiance of Sunny's express wishes – brought his stepmother up to London, to Sunny's own home no less, to meet her: introducing Sunny to Fiona first, *wildly* fallaciously, as "something out of the Necronomicon," and then – rather more accurately, to Sunny's chagrin – as "basically harmless."

"She looks a bit intimidating," he'd added, landing what he must have known would be the coup de grace, "but she's not allowed to hurt anyone. Like, at all."

Sunny had scowled; let her pupils shimmer an unearthly gold and the prongs of her horns break the skin above her brows. To no avail. Fiona, taking Jonas at his word, had been no more afraid of Sunny than she might have been of a smiling capybara floating belly-up by a riverbed. And that lack of fear, that wholesale absence of the kind of healthy respect Sunny is more used to commanding – it has, regrettably, persisted.

"I could break every bone in that foot," she tells Fiona.

"No," Fiona says, not moving from the doorstep, "you couldn't. Now: are you putting the kettle on, or am I?"

The charcoal and hibiscus tea Fiona produces from her mandala-print handbag is undrinkable: better, just, than the seagull wine Sunny once sampled in the Arctic Circle, but worse by some margin than the animal dung blends she enjoyed in the salons of the more health-conscious Victorians.

Fiona, though, seems to delight in it, smacking her lips together appreciatively with every sip.

"Jonas says you've not been getting out much," she

begins, resting her bony elbows on the newly lacquered Pompeii marble of Sunny's dining table.

Sunny remains silent. The less she says, she hopes, the sooner Fiona will be out of her kitchen and back on the street.

"I know how hard it is, losing someone close to you." The witch slurps again at the foul tea. "And it must be so much harder when you're not..." She hesitates. "When you're not used to it. The loss."

The presumptuousness of this riles Sunny; raises her hackles. "I've lived longer than you can possibly imagine," she says. "You have nothing to teach me about loss."

Fiona is unfazed. "Have you had a friend before, though? A proper one, like Miranda?"

The name, or perhaps just hearing it spoken aloud, sharpens the dull twinge in Sunny's chest to a painful point.

"I get the sense from Jonas," the witch continues, "that you'd not had... much to do with people, before her. That you've... kept yourself to yourself a bit. So, no matter *how* old you are, *how* long you've been knocking around – it's going to hurt, isn't it, when someone you care about passes? And Jonas, he won't talk much about what happened to her at the church that night, or to any of those other women you were there with. But I know it must've been bad."

No, Sunny considers – thinking again of *that church* and *that night*, the broken leftovers of her temporary comrades-in-arms among the pews, and the preacher's hand, cloven as a goat's, reaching in to tear Miranda's heart from her flesh before it dropped her to the ground.

Not bad, *Fiona: carnage. A slaughter in a consecrated stockyard.*

I buried the bodies with my own two hands.

"I'm perfectly well," she says, dismissing Fiona's concern

with a roll of her eyes. "Jonas may have neglected to mention it in his recounting of my life story, but I'm quite adept at self-sufficiency. And should I ever feel the need for company, you may rest assured – he and his gentleman-friend are rarely more than a moment away."

"If you say so." The witch doesn't believe her, not for a second, but seems at least to understand the futility of pressing the subject. She sups at the tea; plays absently with the Celtic band around her ring finger. "I really *was* in the area," she adds, draining her cup. "Met up with a couple of the girls in Coventry. Though, alright, yes: I *did* tell Jonas I'd swing by here before I get the train home from Victoria."

"Coventry?" Sunny asks. It's a reflexive query, nothing more. She recalls the place, albeit indistinctly; visited it last in the aftermath of the German War, finding sufficiently little of value among the concrete blocks and rat-infested rubble to warrant any subsequent visits. "Sounds... magical."

"It was interesting, actually. Frustrating, but interesting."

"A hotbed of necromantic enchantment, I'm sure." She pauses; retraces Fiona's previous statement. "Why frustrating?"

"Nothing, really. Just..." Fiona, perhaps sensing the first stirrings of Sunny's curiosity, hesitates. "We've been looking into a couple of... incidents up there. Deaths. We thought there might have been something unusual going on. Something..." She flushes, embarrassed again, then recovers herself. "Oh, sod it. It's *you*, isn't it? You of all people shouldn't need it soft-serving. Something *supernatural*. Magical, if that suits you better."

"Yes?" Sunny raises an eyebrow, urging her to continue – but may already, she thinks, have some vague understanding of the direction in which the subsequent conversation will lead them.

She'd temporarily forgotten this particular proclivity of Fiona's: the predilection she and her cybernated sorceresses have for amateur detection, the solving of imagined crimes. Jonas has been nothing but encouraging of their labours; Sunny, inevitably, has been less so, though how Fiona spends the dwindling seasons of her autumn years is, of course, the witch's own affair. And better sleuthing, she reasons – sleuthing which might furnish Jonas, and by extension Sunny, with a useful or an entertaining anecdote – than beekeeping or poetry-writing or performance art. Sunny has enough raw honey in her cupboards; a surfeit of orchids already on her window sills.

"There were these four lads," Fiona tells her. "*Young* lads – Jonas's age, none of them more than thirty, thirty-five. Never met each other, nothing in common but where they lived. All perfectly healthy, fit and well... until about a month ago, when they started dropping dead. Of *natural causes*, if you can believe that."

Sunny has no reason to *dis*believe it. There are, she's all too aware, a hundred reasons an ostensibly fit youth might suddenly expire in the street, none of them remotely inexplicable: a dormant virus or an undetected illness left untreated; a drug or poison, unheeded by an inattentive medical examiner; a day-old blow to the back of the skull, its impact swept aside even as the blood clots form. *Supernatural* phenomena these are not.

"I see," she says, the brief spark of her interest already fizzling to embers. What exactly will it take for Fiona to grow weary of this little tête-à-tête and propel herself back onto the Euston Road?

"I doubt you do." The old witch sighs, disappointed – or

so it seems to Sunny – with the breadth and reach of her host's imagination. "Whatever you might be thinking... there was nothing normal about the way those kids died. It wasn't talked about in the news, and I expect you can grasp at least why *that* might be. But one of the girls, Lisa, she went to college with the Coroner. They do a sci-fi book club together once a month... Isaac Asimov, that sort of thing. And the way *she* talked about the state of those boys, the state of their bodies... This isn't *natural causes*."

"No?" The embers of Sunny's curiosity, perhaps not quite extinguished after all, flare anew.

"Not unless you think there's something natural about a young lad's brain exploding in his head. And no, that wasn't how the Coroner described it, before you ask – but it's close enough, for here and now. I'm not talking about an aneurysm either, or a few ruptured arteries. Shall I tell you what she *did* tell Lisa, the Coroner? She said nobody'd believe her, if she put it in a report... but it looked to her that something reached in and squeezed those boys' brains by the stem until they burst. Like a grapefruit, she said. Like a bloody grapefruit."

CHAPTER 2

KIRAN

Kiran had never been to a funeral before. Her grandparents were still alive, both sets – one lot in Birmingham, another in Bristol, all of them still working in their seventies – and her aunties and uncles were going strong. Even her mum's brother Chetan, who smoked like a chimney and ate take-away pizza for breakfast. But she'd read they could be cathartic, funerals; that they could give you something like closure.

And if there was one thing she needed right now, it was closure.

The service was out of town, at an old Catholic church in Nuneaton that looked like it should've fallen down already; she'd had to get an early train to make it there for 10am. She hadn't known Dean was Catholic, or his parents were, though she guessed it wasn't the sort of thing you brought up in the office unless you were super religious. Like, *really* into it.

It wasn't a surprise the church was packed: he'd seemed like the sort of bloke who had a lot of friends, who'd been popular at school and kept in touch with all the people in his class. There must've been a hundred people there, squashed together in those narrow wooden seats that left your arse numb if you sat down too long, and most of them about her age – *his* age. She wondered how many of them knew what he was really like: how many of the girls had faked a phone call or a family emergency when he'd come on too strong, refused to take no for an answer. How many of the guys had looked the other way when they could've said something, could've intervened.

More than a few of them, probably. Too many.

She didn't sit down; just stood at the back by the door, next to the little font of holy water, and watched the priest say his prayers and Dean's uncle get up to do a Bible reading. And then it was over.

Six pallbearers carried the coffin outside to the graveyard: five of them strangers, and the sixth her manager, Felipe. Which made sense to Kiran: he and Dean been close, after all. Were old mates; happy to help each other out, when help was needed.

Felipe didn't notice her as he passed, his sights fixed on the sable-suited deltoid of the man in front of him and teeth gritted with the effort of holding up his portion of the coffin's weight. He was short, 5'6 or 7, and she knew it bothered him. He'd be ploughing all his energy into making sure nobody in the crowd thought he was weak – too weak to lower a real man like Dean into the earth – to pay much attention to anyone else.

She stuck around for the burial, which was as brief as she'd hoped it would be, but she didn't scatter with the others when they took off for the wake. She'd wait, she figured: hang out at the back of the church, just out of sight, until even the stragglers had made themselves scarce, then pay her own visit to the graveside. Say her own goodbyes.

She stayed there twenty minutes, playing Angry Birds on her phone and listening to the thrums and mutters of the retreating mourners' voices as they died away to nothing. Then stood up from her bench and slipped back around the corner, towards the hole in the ground where Dean was buried.

Not everyone had left, though. The priest, Dean's family, his friends – they were gone, sure. But there was someone there, still, by the open grave. A white girl, yellow-blonde and younger than Kiran: nineteen or twenty, in dark jeans and a navy sweater and a black fedora with the brim pulled so low it covered her eyes and the top half of her face.

Kiran stopped in her tracks; took a step backwards, then another, until her back hit the crumbling grey brickwork of the church's exterior wall. She wasn't *hidden* – wasn't hiding, either, even if the pooling shadows from the steeple all around her might've made it seem that way. But nor was she conspicuous, exactly; not from where the girl was standing.

In any case, the girl didn't look remotely interested in what was going on around her. She was completely focused instead on the ground in front of her, the ankle-high pile of freshly disturbed earth; was staring, if the tilt and trajectory of her head was any indication, not just *at* the grave, but *into* it. And were her lips moving, too? Kiran couldn't make out any words – or maybe it was just that the girl was whispering – but she definitely seemed to be saying *something*. To Dean; to the body in the box that Dean had been, once.

She brought a thin, pale hand to her face, wiping what must've been tears from her cheeks, and for a second Kiran got a glimpse of her eyes, of the other features hidden under the fedora. Her eye makeup was heavy, the kohl and mascara smeared to panda circle smudges, but she was young – much younger than Kiran had thought originally. A schoolkid: fourteen or fifteen, no older.

Who was she to Dean, then? A niece? A cousin? A best mate's little sister?

She readjusted the fedora, stowing herself away again behind the brim. Lifted her chin, worked her jaw, drew back her shoulders, and spat – two thick, heavy globs of grey saliva – into the open grave.

And then Kiran knew. Maybe not who the girl was, but what she was doing there, at the funeral.

Knew, and understood completely.

CHAPTER 3

SUNNY

There are some ninety miles between Bloomsbury and Coventry – and though both Euston and King's Cross stations are but a brisk walk away from her current abode, Sunny elects to save herself the rail fare and fly to the West Midlands.

A pigeon, she decides, would be the most appropriate body to adopt for such a journey: the aesthetic shortcomings of the form, its jutting breast and comically undersized head, a small price to pay for the comparative inconspicuousness it's apt to afford. Pigeons, after all, are everywhere, particularly in London: a part of the urban furniture, invisible as bollards and the cardboard shelters of the homeless. And pests they may be, to those men and women of the Square Mile on whose designer garments she'll delight in defecating as she takes to the sky – but rarely are they noteworthy. No birdwatcher will stop to track the movements of a pigeon with their eyeglass-telescopes, as they might a goshawk or a peregrine falcon; no trigger-happy airport worker will mistake it for an errant pheasant, should it cross their flight path.

Seen from the pigeon's very literal bird's eye view, London is a Neo-Futurist wonder: a Frank Gehry-ish confection of steel, glass and slow-moving water, as miraculous in its way as Ur and Carthage ever were from overhead. Sunny bores easily, always has, but a changing cityscape observed over millennia may be the closest thing she's known to a reliable source of pleasure – each new iteration yet another image-frame, another strip of reel to be added to the moving picture building in her immaculate memory.

If only, she thinks – as she soars, wings spread, over St. Pancras – she were able to rid herself of her propensity for boredom; of that implacable curiosity and unquenchable neophilia that propelled her so frequently to wander place to place, entirely rootless, in the times before Miranda and the preacher. Perhaps *then*, she might have found the bait Fiona set for her a little less alluring. The old witch had been clever, bringing her tale of grisly, peculiar death to Sunny's door – Sunny would grant her that. The bloodshed; the gratifying tragedy of young men struck down in their prime; the implicit challenge of an *unsolved mystery* with preternatural overtones... anyone familiar with Sunny would know she'd find the combination irresistible. And Jonas, of course, already knew Sunny better than most.

That Jonas put his stepmother up to it; that he encouraged Fiona not only to *check in on* Sunny but to tempt her to visit Coventry and appraise the situation for herself... this, for Sunny, is a foregone conclusion. He's a sensitive boy, despite the newly acquired magicks that course through him, and he gives every indication, absurd though Sunny finds the idea, of actually caring for her – for Sunny's peace of mind, *her wellbeing*. And he's expressed concerns of late about her aimlessness, and what he so earnestly calls her *lack of purpose* – albeit principally to his paramour, the soon-to-be Mr Jonas, when neither were aware they could be heard.

Enter: Fiona, and the intractable Problem of the Detonated Heads. The perfect puzzle to occupy Sunny, to keep her purposefully distracted in his absence.

It's infuriating, that a ruse so transparent should have proven so successful – should have worked on her so undeniably well. And yet, here she is: a thousand feet and rising over London, en route to a location altogether less auspicious, in pursuit of an inhuman criminal mastermind who may not, in fact, exist at all.

Infuriating. Utterly, utterly infuriating.

She lands on the roof of a very large, unnecessarily grandiose country house tucked away in the corner of a farming village six miles northwest of Coventry proper: the kind of place that's apt to call itself The Priory or The Old Vicarage, whatever its lineage. There's a tennis court, she observes; an outdoor swimming pool and a sunken croquet lawn; five acres of wooded field and carefully cultivated land separating the property from its nearest neighbour.

On the roof, unseen, she changes: her wings condensing down to paws, her talons to hind legs, her feathered tail to a longer, thinner model insulated by sleek black fur. Feline rather than avian, she crosses the roof and begins her descent – window to lintel, window to lintel – until finally she leaps, landing lightly on the stone-lined path before the high front door.

Once securely tethered to the ground, she changes a second time, reverting to what might be considered her *original* body: the blue-skinned, bipedal form in which she was cast, in the beginning. No sense, she thinks, in pretending to be other than she is; not here, out of sight, among her own kind.

She can feel them everywhere, the ones like her, just as she imagines *they* can feel *her*: their presence a scattering of pock-like disruptions in the magnetic field-map by which she navigates this world. They don't enjoy one another's company, exactly. Nor do they make a point of seeking one another out for any reason but the practical. But they know who they are, and *where* they are. Moreover, and perhaps most importantly: every one of them, Sunny included, is bound by the same set of rules, on this particular plane. Rules consecrated – and enforced; so strictly and so readily enforced – in their *own* world. Forbidding them from harming any human by their own hand; from allowing those same humans to venture where they ought not, beyond the bounds of their Earth.

And, of course – from refusing hospitality and haven to one another, should either be requested.

It's in the knowledge of a certain guaranteed welcome, therefore – if not necessarily a *warm* one – that Sunny knocks at the door.

The creature who opens it wears the shape and skin of a curvaceous, apple-cheeked human woman in her fourth decade: the complexion pale pink, the hair a mass of light-brown ringlets, the green eyes lit with mischief. She wears a tight turquoise tunic, gold pendant earrings and sandals on her feet, a variation on the same outfit – and indeed the same body – she's worn, to the best of Sunny's recollection, since the fall of the Ptolemaic Kingdom.

As modern as she may fancy herself, Sunny thinks, she never *did* get over Cleopatra.

"Ah," the creature greets her, in the old language. "It's you."

"And a pleasure it is, as always," Sunny replies, slipping herself into their shared tongue.

She knows, without needing to ask – much as she knew where to find the house and its resident – that the creature goes by *Bunny*, here and now: a bastardisation of the Macedonian-Hellenic *Berenice*.

Together, she thinks – reflecting on her own moniker, the one Miranda gave her – they're practically a cabaret troupe: *The Sunny and Bunny Comedy Hour*.

"I was hoping," she adds, "you might have room for a guest, these next few days."

Bunny grimaces, cornered, then rallies, rearranging her features into a smile.

"How could I refuse?" she tells Sunny, and opens the door wider to let her inside.

Inside, the house really *could* be an Old Vicarage. Bunny's furniture is cheap wood, mid-20th century, and smells faintly of furniture polish; her curtains and upholstery suggest material repurposed from old clothes gathered during England's post-war rationing period. In the cavernous kitchen into which she leads them, a bronze lamp hangs over an open fireplace, neither of them particularly well-crafted despite their advanced age; in the hallway Sunny notices a tarnished suit of armour, Tudor or Stuart, that even she considers incongruous.

Bunny offers no explanation for these aesthetic decisions, offensive though she must realise they are. Rather, she busies herself with a performance of conviviality, brewing coffee and laying the table with mille-feuille and macarons, both more agreeable by far than the decor that surrounds them.

"And how long were you thinking of staying?" she asks Sunny, adding spoon after spoon of thickly stiffening cream into her cup. "I only ask, because I've been messing around with the Shakespeare Society over in Midgrove, and we've got rehearsals for Twelfth Night on every night next week in the run-up to the show. I'm Olivia," she adds, with what seems to Sunny wholly unwarranted pride.

Bunny always *did* like people, Sunny remembers. Always enjoyed their company, their fellowship; was more protective of them, individually and as a genus, than Sunny was ever prepared to be. Even in the Old Times, she spent more of her days among them here than she did back home.

Moreover, unlike Sunny, she's never seemed to crave their adulation, their worship: has never, to Sunny's knowledge, sat at the head of a cult or taken offerings of gold at a purpose-built temple.

Sunny can't imagine why not.

"No more than a few days," she says, keeping her answer vague – aware that the possibility of a prolonged house-call will drive Bunny to distraction, and caring not a whit.

"Lovely." A part of Sunny has to admire the authenticity of Bunny's performance, her beautifully rendered but surely manufactured sincerity. She may give the Midgrove Shakespeare Society their finest Olivia yet. "And what brings you to the Midlands?"

"Murder. Or should I say, murders. Suspicious deaths, at the very least."

Bunny nods, new understanding dawning. Sunny always did have a nose for a bloodbath; was renowned for it, once.

"Those boys down in Cofa's Tree," Bunny says, sagely -

the Anglo-Saxon nomenclature better suited to the old tongue, Sunny thinks, than *Coventry*.

"Quite so. You know of them?"

"How could I not? They've been the talk of the town."

"You've identified the guilty party, then?" Sunny asks.

She nibbles at her macaron expectantly; notes awkwardness passing like a summer storm cloud over Bunny's cheery tavern wench visage. Clearly, the guilty party has *not* been identified, the villain *not* unmasked on Bunny's watch; clearly Bunny, up to her neck in this Saint Mary Mead pantomime of am-dram and home-baked scones, has as much insider insight to add to Fiona's PI dossier as a week-old local newspaper clipping.

It's fun, nevertheless, to watch her squirm.

"I'm afraid I haven't... probed," Bunny admits, after a moment. "Is it something *we* ought to be interested in, do you think?"

Sunny fixes her with a knowing, three-eyed stare, feeling suddenly like Hercule Poirot, setting out to solve the mystery of the disappearing Clapham Cook.

"That," she says, "remains to be seen."

And finishes her macaron.

CHAPTER 4

ANAND

He started to feel funny on the walk home: dizzy and lightheaded, unsteady on his feet. Probably he was hungry, Anand thought. Knackered from work, and physically drained from running around after too many customers. He needed to eat something, that was all. Get something in his stomach before he passed out.

Tasha had dinner on the table when he walked in: lasagne and garlic bread, ice cream and profiteroles for after. All of it shop-bought; not her best. He ate it, obviously, but without any real enthusiasm.

"There's a new art thing in town," he said, after he'd cleaned his plate. "One of those... what do you call them? Installations. Augmented reality, holograms and that, out near the shopping centre. Figured you might be into it."

It was a safe bet. She'd done art at college, hadn't she? And she'd spent ages playing that Pokémon game on her phone when she thought he wasn't watching.

Although, now he stopped to think about it: *was* it art, what he'd seen? It was weird enough to *be* art – look at that giant floating baby he'd seen the time they went to Singapore, or those garden gnomes on the island out by Salford Quays. But maybe it was a marketing stunt; some London bloke's idea of advertising, trying to sell him... something. He wished now he'd studied it harder, really taken in the details. But it had sprung at him so quickly, out of nowhere, like that 3D shark poster jumping out at Marty McFly from the Jaws 19 poster in *Back to the Future* – so unexpectedly he'd nearly pissed himself. And the shock of it had given him a headache that had made his ears ring. He still hadn't managed to shake it off.

He'd take a couple of ibuprofen tablets once he finished eating, he decided. Wash them down with a San Miguel, maybe a spliff. Then bed; an early night, no telly.

"A hologram?" Tash said. "You sure? Nadia didn't say anything about a hologram, and she's..."

She stopped herself abruptly, seeming to realise all at once what she'd let slip.

"Nadia?" He didn't raise his voice. Maybe he wouldn't need to. "You spoke to her?"

"No!" The reply came quick; too quick and too loud, the surest sign that she was covering her tracks. "I mean, she called, before. But she was only on for a minute, and I didn't *want* to talk to her, she just..."

He put down the glass he'd been holding; slowly, gently. "But you picked up. When she called."

She was a fucking bitch, Nadia. And she *hated* Anand; had done since the night they'd met, when he and Tash had had that row about the bloke at the bar who'd been trying it on. She'd never bothered to pretend otherwise, either: she'd been on at Tash for *days* when Anand had asked her to move in with him. Warning her off him; telling her to wait a bit, that there was no harm in taking her time.

He'd known what *that'd* meant, even if he hadn't known exactly what the bitch had said to Tash, or how she'd said it.

Tash hadn't listened to her, obviously. And he'd believed her when she told him Nadia was history – that it was *him* she cared about, not her, and *of course* she wouldn't carry on being mates with someone who talked about her bloke that way.

More fool him.

He stood up from the table, his hands already curling into fists. She took a step backwards, then another, like she was trying to get away from him. Like she was scared of him.

Scared of him, for fuck's sake.

His guts churned, and he felt his whole body flush hot and cold, the way it always did right before he lost his rag. His head throbbed, the pressure rising in his scalp and in his eardrums.

"Please, babe," she said, still backing away. "Let's just sit down on the sofa and chill, yeah? Put something on Netflix and just... relax a bit."

"I don't want to watch fucking Netflix," he growled. It was a tsunami now, the pain; like water building up behind a dam.

"What about we go out a bit, then? Nip outside for a walk, or... Jesus *Christ*." She froze; stared at him. "What *is* that, coming out your eyes?"

His eyes? What did his eyes *have to do with anything?*

Unconsciously, he touched two fingers to his face, to the corner of one eye. They came away wet and red; bloody.

"Where did...?" he started. Everything was blurry, suddenly. Distorted.

Then the dam burst, and all he heard was Tasha screaming.

CHAPTER 5

SUNNY

There's no use in approaching the town centre in any form but human: she'd be spotted, and remarked upon, the moment she began to change, and the undivided attention of a bevy of gawping onlookers is the very last thing she needs, just at present.

Besides, Bunny has a car, an absurdly old convertible with no discernible roof, that looks as if it might once have belonged to Henry Ford himself. She seems content enough to take it for a spin, and Sunny with it.

They navigate the curving backroads of the rural Midlands in a quasi-silence, Bunny humming snatches of a long-forgotten murder ballad to herself as she spins the wheel. At Sunny's request, she releases her guest into the very epicentre of the city, beside a bustling public square funnelling tired-eyed townsfolk into an American-style shopping complex Sunny would rather crucify herself than enter.

Sunny exits the vehicle without bidding her goodbye.

The smell of fried dough lingers in the air: donuts or jalebi, though Sunny herself prefers a sopaipilla. Pigeons, underwhelming in their morphic fixity, peck with enthusiasm at the paving stones; office workers chained by polyester lanyards cluster in twos and threes around a statue of a naked woman on horseback, sucking with an infant's satisfaction at the whistle-like tubes so many of them take to now for comfort, in the absence of tobacco.

She recognises the naked woman, if not the horse. It's Godgifu, if memory serves. Or rather, in the Newer Englishes, Godiva: Lady of Mercia, naked equestrian, scourge of voyeurs far and wide. Sunny never knew her personally – *her* 11th century was spent for the most part in Tamilakam among the Cholas, a dynasty altogether more receptive to her charms than the priestly Normans and purse-lipped Sasanachs assailing England. But she was aware enough of the legends, as they swelled and replicated over time: the Tennyson poem and the Peeping Tom effigies and the children's rhymes about *fine ladies* and Banbury Cross.

Godiva is an odd choice of icon for a city to commemorate, Sunny thinks – but then, who's to say what other options the aldermen of Cofa's Tree had to choose from? Better an exhibitionist than an Elizabeth Báthory, certainly from a tourism perspective.

She tarries by the glass storefront of a footwear retailer, her gaze passing rapidly from one display to another – boot to boot, running shoe to running shoe. Might *she* benefit, she wonders, from a pair of soft-soled plimsolls, if she's to persist in this form for the duration of her stay? Her own feet, cloven as they are, require little in the way of maintenance, beyond the occasional prune with a trimming shear. But human feet are less durable, more easily damaged; the human forms she adopts, though always ostensibly clothed, are as illusory as mirages in the desert, offering only the *appearance* of comfort; and the deerskin moccasins she purloined from the wardrobe of Bunny's guest bedroom will, she predicts, quickly prove impractical in this city of paving bricks and cobblestones.

Later, perhaps.

In dribs and drabs, the not-quite-smokers depart their perch, drifting like so many clouds of vapour towards their offices, their computer terminals and fax machines.

(*Printers*, she can almost hear Miranda tell her – not quite daring to mock Sunny outright for her technological ignorance. *They use printers now, not fax machines. And mostly they don't bother with the printed word at all*).

Inspired by the dynamism around her, low-key though it is, she tears herself away from the storefront and orients herself towards her destination: an apartment block a minute from the shopping centre, olive-brown and cheaply-made, upwardly-mobile aspiration seeping from the tough-ened laminate pores of its every Juliet balcony.

Her *mark*, as she's sure Fiona would say, is one Naomi Foy, the present and as of late *only* occupant of Flat 27. Foy, Sunny has gleaned from the witch's case notes, is thirty-one years old; a Tae Kwon Do brown belt and regular marathon runner, though quite why Fiona considered *those* details worthy of inclusion, Sunny couldn't begin to fathom. The girl is an actuary by trade; a former student of contour fashion design, which Sunny gathers predominantly involves the construction of corsetry and undergarments; and, most saliently in this instance, the newly widowed spouse of *Jonathan* Foy – third victim of whatever or whomever has been killing off the men of the southernmost West Midlands.

The apartment block has, of course, a wrought-iron security gate and intercom system, but Sunny had expected nothing less, and has, fortuitously, rather a knack for circumnavigating such impediments. A flick of the wrist, a click of the fingers, and the gate unfastens; thereafter, she need only persuade the steel lock on the entryway into the lobby to relinquish its hold and hike the two-and-a-half flights of dustily-carpeted stair, past three framed reproductions of the same Mondrian canvas, before she's at Naomi and the former Jonathan Foy's front door, her own – figurative – notebook poised to receive whatever new evidence she unearths within.

Naomi Foy, she discovers as the door flies open, is the kind of woman others might consider intimidating. She's tall for a human, six feet at least in flat-heeled loafers, and possesses the jutting chin and sneering swagger of a Timur or a Henry VIII: a full-grown playground bully, conquering the objects in her orbit through sheer, aggressive force of will.

"How did you get in without buzzing?" she says. She's Irish; Ulster, Sunny believes, and might Fiona not have included *that* little detail in her precis of the situation? Impossible these days for Sunny to hear that accent without thinking of Miranda; of their first strange, gore-drenched meeting in the woods of Donegal, so long ago now, Naomi Foy's great-grandmother would scarcely have been born. Miranda had lost all but the faintest traces of the dialect over the years, by accident or choice, but when every now and then she dropped her guard, Sunny could hear the inflections, all the same: the peaks and the eddies of it, the rhotic *r*s and unexpected plosives.

"You listening?" Naomi Foy glares at her, her shoulders squaring in the spirit of pre-emptive confrontation. "I said, how did you get in here, and what do you want? You're supposed to use the intercom, not barge straight into the building."

Honestly, Sunny thinks, pitying for a moment the woman's friends and junior colleagues, those poor unfortunates with no option but to entertain her rudeness. *Must everything forever be so* challenging?

"I'm a police... person," she says. A clear and obvious lie, but the most complex cover story she can muster the energy to assemble. "I'd like to talk to you about your husband, Jonathan. I understand he... left us recently?"

"ID?" Naomi Foy believes not a word of the subterfuge, and on that particular point – if no other – Sunny can hardly blame her.

She begins the charade of hunting in the inner pocket of Bunny's preposterous and entirely un-detective-like sheepskin jacket for a warrant card, a wallet, an NYPD officer's badge and shield, anything at all that might fit the bill... and then, exhausted by the effort, gives up the performance altogether, electing to fall back on the magicks. She waves a hand before Naomi Foy's incredulous face; whispers a smattering of thrall-words in the mother tongue, the ones that never fail her.

The old ways are the best ways, even now.

Naomi Foy's demeanour shifts immediately to helpful deference. "Sorry," she tells Sunny. "Come in, of course. Wile cold, you must be, standing out there."

She reverses, letting Sunny pass.

The apartment is as cold and unforgiving as Naomi Foy herself: so thoroughly pared-back Sunny wonders, until she catches sight of the white leather three-piece suite in the open-plan living/dining/office space, whether the Foys had decided to dispense altogether with the need for furniture.

Unbidden, Sunny seats herself on the sofa. Naomi only hovers in the centre of the room, paralysed by uncertainty.

Eventually, Sunny relents.

"Sit," she says – and, grateful, Naomi Foy obeys.

"Now." Sunny rests an elbow on the sofa's armrest, which squeaks like cheese-curd at her touch. "What can you tell me about your husband... imploding?"

She'd skimmed the incident reports before she left London; interpreted them as a supplement to the more fulsome and altogether more breathless descriptions of crushed organs and cerebrospinal fluid seepage Fiona's e-coven had passed along from their coroner friend. But it never hurt to hear these things first-hand – and Naomi Foy, Sunny has been given to understand, was here, at the scene of the crime, in the very moment of the hapless Jonathan's expiration.

"What do you want to know?" Naomi asks, a fresh note of anxiety splintering the edges of her voice.

"Everything," Sunny says. "Absolutely everything."

There is, as it transpires, little left for the widow Foy to tell. Little, in any event, that Sunny hadn't gleaned already from her background reading.

Jonathan Foy, returning from a lunch date with his brother one ordinary Tuesday three weeks earlier, had begun complaining of a headache; a condition for which Naomi, studying for her latest batch of actuarial examinations at the standing desk they shared, had, at least initially, little sympathy.

"I thought he'd been out on the lash," she tells Sunny. "Him and Craig – day-drinking, you know? It always happened, with the two of them together. But then his nose started bleeding, proper pouring with it, and he was coughing up globs of this thick red shite, all over the floor, and then…"

And *then*, like the others, he'd collapsed: dropped to the floor, blood gushing not only from his nose and mouth but from his ears and eyeballs too, and begun to convulse, twitching and flopping like a line-caught haddock until eventually, lips foaming and nostrils already half-congealed, he'd lain still.

"I rang 999," Naomi Foy adds – though the strength of the protestation leads Sunny to wonder just how *long* she'd waited before pressing the Call button. "I did. But it was ages, like, before they bothered to turn up, even after I told them the state Johnny was in. And when they did get here… well, there was fuck all they could do, wasn't there? Anyone with eyes could see he was gone."

"Why wasn't he at work that day?" Sunny says. If Agatha Christie and the Golden Age detectives have taught her anything, it's that the solving of crime depends on the capturing of the smallest details, however inconsequential they might at first appear. Jonathan Foy, she knows, was a dentist in life: an endodontist, specialising in the diagnosis and treatment of abscesses and the provision of root canals to a select roster of private patients. Such men, in her experience, are not often to be found taking long midweek lunches or lounging about their sitting-rooms at 2pm on a Tuesday. Moreover, could she – or indeed *Naomi* Foy – *really* be sure he was dining with his brother that day? Might he have been meeting instead with a lover, or a drug-dealer, or a business partner leading him, unbeknown to his wife, into a labyrinth of shady backstreet dealings? And were that the case: might that lover or that drug-dealer or that business partner have been motivated to slip a vial of poison – tasteless, colourless and untraceable – into J. Foy's glass of wine, his decaffeinated Grande macchiato?

There are so very many possibilities.

"He'd been suspended," Naomi Foy replies – still thralled, still compliant, but sounding suddenly venomous. "The partners at his practice, Keenan and that gobshite Delisle... they'd put him on leave. *Unpaid*, obviously." She sneers; not at Sunny, but at the recollection, as if the memory of a bad smell has unexpectedly assailed her.

"On leave?" Sunny senses the thread of an investigative string, one at which she might gently tug.

"Yeah." Venom, hot and pure, suffuses the widow Foy's features. "Told Johnny they *had to do it*, after what that boss-eyed bitch on reception said he'd done to her. That he'd *left them with no choice*. As if either one of them believed the bullshit she was spinning, believed he'd even *look* at her twice, the way she was, with *those* teeth, and that greasy rat-tail hair all the way to her arse." The widow takes a deep, theatrical breath: no longer speaking to Sunny, but addressing instead an invisible courtroom, a hypothetical jury of her peers. "You tell me, now: what would a good-looking fella like Johnny be doing sticking a camera up the skirt of a runty little thing like *that*?"

CHAPTER 6

KIRAN

It was her mum, of all people, who told her there'd been another one.

"Have you seen this?" she asked Kiran, shoving the local paper under her daughter's nose, a ghoulish excitement thickening her voice to a nasal Brummie. "Another young lad dropped dead just up the road. Younger than you."

Kiran's stomach tightened; panic – the same panic she'd felt all the *other* times it had happened – bringing what seemed like every drop of blood in her body to the surface of her skin.

"Yeah?" she said, batting the paper away and manoeuvring herself towards the kitchen door, beyond maternal reach. "Weird."

Harpreet Nagra, however, was not so easily evaded, least of all by her firstborn.

"It's a bloody worry," she continued, following Kiran out into the hallway. "Twenty-one years old, this lad. Only just out of uni. He could've been at school with your brother."

"What did he die of?" Kiran stalled by the stairs,

avoiding her mum's eye but wanting details despite herself. Despite the very real possibility she knew the answer, or *some* of the answer, already.

"Sudden Adult Death Syndrome - that's what they're calling it." Harpreet waved the paper for emphasis. "Same as the others. No illness, no mention of drugs... nothing. One minute he's out for a run on the park, and the next..."

She mimed cutting her own throat. Kiran winced.

"What was his name?" The question was out of her mouth before she could stop it.

Stupid. So fucking stupid. Whatever it was, whichever one of them *he* was – he'd be the last thing she thought about before she fell asleep tonight. Him and Dean and the rest of them.

"Hang on." Harpreet glanced down at the paper; scanned the columns below the headline. "There." She pointed a finger at a line of text. "Niall. Niall Watson. From Newcastle, it says. Moved here for college. Was about to start his training contract at Marlowe and Green – that big firm next to the cinema, across from your dad's office."

Niall Watson. The photo of the blue-eyed, floppy-haired, generically pretty white boy staring back at her from the front page of the Herald meant nothing to Kiran; she could've walked past him a dozen times in the street without it registering.

"Kiran?" She tore herself away from the picture. Saw her mum was watching her – with growing concern, if the crease between Harpreet's eyebrows was any indication. "You alright? You were miles away."

"Fine." Kiran forced a smile; let her face settle into the lie. "Totally fine."

She ran upstairs the first chance she got, away from her mum and the Herald and the follow-up conversation that would no doubt ensue when her dad got home from work, full of feigned sadness and genuine curiosity about the new kid's death and the deaths that had preceded it. He knew people at Marlowe and Green; they all knew each other, solicitors. He wouldn't have met Niall Watson, wouldn't have had a chance to – but he'd know someone who had.

He *had* met Dean, briefly – just once, when Kiran and Dean had bumped into him in town on their way to get a coffee one lunchtime. But she hadn't introduced them, hadn't given her dad Dean's name – and Dean's death, anyway, hadn't made the news. Not even locally.

There hadn't been a story to report on, then. Hadn't been a pattern.

Dean, he'd been the first.

Safe in her room, a suitcase full of old sketch pads shoved against the door to keep either parent from barging in, she dug the book out from under the bed. It felt just as unpleasant to touch as it had before: too soft and too warm, the brown leather binding like a living thing under her hands. It wasn't possible, she knew that – but it felt, somehow, like the covers were moving, undulating. Breathing, even. It sickened her a bit, just holding it.

She didn't have much choice, though, did she?

She opened it up to the page she'd bookmarked. The lines she'd sought out, that first time; the ones she'd thought would help her.

That *had* helped her, she supposed. In a way.

But it had gone too far now. Dean was one thing: she'd known, with him, exactly what she wanted, what she was getting into. These other lads, though – she'd never even met them.

Whatever it was that was happening, whatever she'd started – it had to be stopped.

She just had to figure out how.

CHAPTER 7

SUNNY

Even under duress, Bunny's will to host shines bright enough to dazzle the unwary.

Just this morning – without so much as asking whether Sunny has an appetite – she's rustled up a breakfast banquet vast enough to bring tears to the eye of a Medici wedding planner. There is pork, of course: bacon, and sausages, and lardons and black pudding, luxuriating in their fat. There are kippers and salmon; fried potatoes and kidney beans and ripe avocados and congee; eggs prepared to every conceivable specification. There is coconut rice in banana leaf; yoghurt and honey; borek and baklava.

And there is coffee, flowing fast and thick as the Nile itself from a tall, long-handled copper pot Sunny is sure she once saw displayed in the British Museum.

"Will you be speaking to the girl today, do you think?" Bunny asks, helping herself to a spoonful of shakshuka. "The dental receptionist?" She's doing the best she can to frame her interest in Sunny's detective work as polite inquiry and nothing more, but she's chomping at the bit for particulars, and the more salacious the better. Sunny can tell.

Not even the Midgrove Shakespeare Society, Sunny thinks, can deliver gossip quite so satisfying as this.

"This afternoon," she says, cleaning chilli oil from the bottom of her plate with a slab of brioche. "I plan to visit the surgery after I've dropped in on Natasha Larkin. Anand Kumar's live-in paramour."

"Anand Kumar?" Bunny feigns ignorance, though Sunny is certain she recalls the man, or at the very least Sunny's mention of him the previous evening. She's fishing for details; goading Sunny into offering up a little more gore, a soupçon more blood and brain matter over this morning's repast.

Sunny, however, will not be playing ball.

"Another of our victims," she answers, neutrally. "Miss Larkin was the last to see him before he expired. I thought perhaps she might have something of interest to say."

"Sounds to me like the first girl might be the more useful of the two, if it's motive you're looking for." Bunny prods at the shakshuka before her with a dessert fork. "Upskirting photos? More than reason enough to knock off that dentist, I should say."

"The *dentist*, yes." Sunny shakes her head, already regretting sharing with Bunny even these earliest of her findings. "But you forget, dear – we have five other victims to contend with. I doubt very much that *all* of them came after our receptionist with a telephoto lens. And that's leaving aside the rather pressing question of *how* she could have killed them, were she thus disposed."

"I suppose." Bunny swallows her egg and chews, her face contemplative. "Still, though. Sneaking *those* sorts of pictures? I may not have met your Mr Foy, but his removal, whoever *did* remove him, doesn't strike me as too terrible a loss, at the macro level. I might even call it a net *good*, if we're being consequentialist about it."

The presence of this moralistic streak in a creature like Bunny strikes *Sunny* as inordinately comical. But she can't dispute the wider point. Jonathan Foy – husband, dentist, sexual predator – does seem to have been a singularly repugnant man; his prior work history scarred and potholed, as Sunny discovered following her conversation with the widow Foy, with never-quite-proven allegations and rescinded accusations of misconduct. She can think of few better candidates for an impromptu head-explosion. Should the receptionist turn out after all to have orchestrated his death, Sunny – and by the sounds of things, Bunny – would be rather more inclined to take her out for dinner than surrender her to the authorities.

"Let's wait and see what Miss Larkin has to add to the mix, shall we?" Sunny tears another hearty chunk of brioche from the loaf and swirls it around the remaining oil. "Who knows? Perhaps she and the receptionist are in it together. Perhaps they made a pact – like *Strangers on a Train*, you know? Extinguishing the not-so-eligible men of Cofa's Tree, one chancing levereter at a time."

Bunny shakes her head once more and reaches for the stolen coffee pot. "Is there *nothing* you take seriously?" she says, and clucks her tongue at Sunny like a reproachful mother hen.

Natasha Larkin seems to Sunny, at first blush, the very opposite of Naomi Foy: a small-framed, fine-boned porcelain doll of a girl, afraid of her own shadow.

Like Naomi Foy, she is hesitant initially to invite Sunny into the cramped Victorian terrace she shared until very recently with Anand Kumar – requiring Sunny to concoct another, equally implausible account vis-à-vis her visit to the Larkin-Kumar residence, and to buttress this explanation with a further dusting of thrall.

*Un*like the widow Foy, Natasha Larkin is anything but combative in response to Sunny's probing.

"He was so *angry* all the time," she says of her departed lover, not only compliant but actively effusive – as if an unacknowledged part of her has been desperate since his death to share a portion of her story, and Sunny's small influence has done nothing but release the stopper. "I don't know what it was that pissed him off. His job, or his family, or if he was just *like* that. He'd come home raging, though: shouting and smashing things and punching walls. He was sweet as anything when he calmed down," she adds quickly, leaving Sunny to wonder whether even her *unconscious* mind recoils at the prospect of doling out criticism. "I don't want you thinking he was a monster. He wasn't. He was a nice bloke, a kind bloke. But... yeah. He scared me a bit, when he got like that. You couldn't talk to him, couldn't get him to listen, couldn't say anything right. You just had to wait for whatever was rattling him to... burn itself out. Or something. You know what I mean?"

Sunny nods, a mimeograph of empathetic understanding. It's interesting, she thinks, that Anand Kumar should *also* have been so flawed, so unpleasant. Might there be a behavioural pattern at play here, after all? Might this propensity to abuse the women in their lives be the very thread connecting Foy and Kumar – and the other victims, too?

"And he was... angry with you, the evening he died?" she

asks. Perhaps this line of enquiry will prove relevant, and perhaps it won't, but Sunny is hardly up against a deadline. She can afford, for now, to be a little expansive in her questioning.

"Yeah." Natasha Larkin looks down at her long, turquoise-lacquered nails, embarrassed. It's an embarrassment laced with self-loathing, a strand of shame that Sunny recognises. She's seen it before, and often, in the downtrodden and the subjugated; in the face, until these last few decades, of every other woman she surveyed in every land she passed through.

What's wrong with you, that he should do this? That you should let *him do this?*

"And this anger, you find it... noteworthy? Related to what happened to him, somehow?"

"No!" On this point, Natasha Larkin is vehement. "God, no. I thought for a minute, when it started – the bleeding and that – that maybe he'd, I don't know... brought it on himself. Got himself so worked up he'd ruptured something, somewhere. But it wasn't that; it couldn't've been. There was something up with him before any of that kicked off. Something other than him being livid. The way he was acting, the stuff he was saying, from when he walked in the front door that night... it was *weird*. He wasn't himself."

"No?" *Weirdness*, in Sunny's not-inconsiderable experience, is *always* an avenue worthy of exploration.

"No." The girl continues to study her nails, absorbed by their sparkle. There are patterns drawn on them, Sunny sees now: yellow whorls and scratches against their blue-green backdrop, each nail a rendering of Van Gogh's Starry Night in microcosm "He was telling me about something he'd seen out in town. A hologram installation thing. Public art, he said... though it could've been an advert, I suppose. One of those ones you see jumping out at you from billboards in Leicester Square. Only… there *wasn't* a hologram there that day, not here in Cov. I googled it after, had a search around online, and there was just… nothing. No photos, no videos, no-one even *mentioning* they'd seen it, and it's exactly the kind of thing you'd expect everyone to be talking about and taking pictures of, or what's the point of pulling a stunt like that in the first place? AR and VR and holograms and whatever – they're there to be looked at, aren't they? It's theatre, all of it. Doesn't matter if it's a new pair of trainers you're selling or an exhibition at the Tate Modern. But Anand, whatever he thought he saw – it *wasn't there*. Wasn't real."

"I see," Sunny says – seeing nothing concrete, not yet, but inclined to let Natasha Larkin talk on regardless, lest some further and more obvious clue reveal itself in the meandering.

"The police said there was nothing in his system, when they tested him," the girl adds. "Nothing that would've made him see things, made him hallucinate. But drugs, they're not the only things that bring on hallucinations, are they? Head injuries can do it, too. And I know there weren't any… what did they say at the hospital? Any *visible signs of trauma* on him, besides the blood. But what if something *did* hit him when he was coming home from work, or ran into him, and the doctors and that missed whatever it was when they were examining him? Or what if got into it with someone in the street on his way back, and they lamped him, and *that* brought on the bleeding in his brain afterwards? You get that sometimes, don't you, a delayed reaction? He didn't mention a fight, or anyone going for him – but like I said, he got angry, sometimes. And not just at me."

Sunny makes a mental note to examine more closely Anand Kumar's personal history: an arrest record or two, no doubt, lurks somewhere in those annals. She anticipates the shape of them: the log upon log of petty violences inflicted, so prosaic and so *predictable* they'd lead Bunny – sensitive, hopeful Bunny – to weep for the state of humanity.

These apparent *hallucinations* of Kumar's, though – they might yet be worth pursuing, too. There are more things in heaven and earth, Sunny knows, that can be dreamt of via Instagram and street photography. Others may not have seen or heard – or documented – whatever phenomenon the boy reported to Natasha Larkin on his deathbed. But that's no reason at all to suppose it *wasn't there* and *didn't happen*.

"This hologram," she asks. "Where was Anand exactly, when he saw it?"

CHAPTER 8
RICH

He'd hit the heavy bag hard, just then; too hard, probably. Hadn't wrapped his hands up before he started, either: was too frustrated, too fucking *angry* to bother hunting around in his locker for his bandages or gloves. His wrists and knuckles were going to kill him tomorrow. His shins wouldn't be far behind, either, the way he'd gone for it with those roundhouse kicks.

Usually he felt energised after a bag-work session: fired up, ready to sprint home and play hopscotch over every paving slab he passed along the way. It was disappointing, then, to find himself so deflated, even after ninety minutes of dripping sweat onto the mat.

He knew why; of course he did. Why he couldn't shake it off, that sick defeated feeling he'd brought with him into the gym. Whose fault it was he'd felt that way in the first place.

It was her – all her.

Zara.

Okay: so maybe he *did* cross a line, like she said, turning up outside her office like that. And probably he shouldn't have told the bloke at the front desk he was her brother –

he could see why someone who didn't know the situation might've thought that was a bridge too far. But she hadn't answered his texts or DMs, hadn't replied to any of the emails he'd sent to the address he'd found on her LinkedIn, so what else was he supposed to do to get her to talk to him?

He'd remembered her mentioning a brother, the night they'd met. Jerome? Jeremy? Something like that. She hadn't said where he lived, or if he was even in the country – the guy could've been in Dubai, for all Rich knew. But it seemed a safe enough bet she'd make the journey down from whichever floor she worked on to see him, if he rocked up out of the blue.

Rich had judged *that* right, at least.

The look on her face when she saw him, though – when she realised it was *Rich* standing there, and not Jerome or Jeremy or whoever. The confusion, then the realisation once she clocked who the person she'd come to meet actually was. And after that, the fear, the disgust: like Rich was a serial killer about to come at her with a carving knife. That was going to haunt him for a long, long time.

Because what had Rich ever done, to make her think that? All he'd wanted was to talk to her, for them to get to know each other. There'd been something between them that night in the pub, hadn't there? Something real. She'd felt it, just as much as he had. Why *wouldn't* she want to give it a chance?

"That's not my brother." That was all she'd said, there in the lobby, before she'd turned around and walked right back into the lift. And not even to Rich – to the man at the desk, the receptionist. She must've known what would happen next: that the old bloke would beckon over the security guards who'd been lingering by the revolving doors in their too-tight suits and have Rich chucked out onto the pavement.

Be thankful it's us doing this and not the police, after what you just did, the big African one had told him, when Rich had shouted at the dude to let go of his arm, to stop touching him.

You want to listen to him, the other one had chimed in – the white one, a chubby little fuck with a Cockney accent that made him sound like Bob Hoskins. *Can't just go around bothering girls while they're at work, can you? Harassment, that is.*

If someone did that to one of my *daughters,* the first one added, *he'd be going home on crutches, I can promise you that.*

But the man's grip on Rich's elbow was already loosening, and Rich had pulled himself free enough to make a run for it. He hadn't *stopped* running until he'd got to the cathedral – and only then to catch his breath.

Bastards.

He picked up his pace: heading away from the gym, the humiliation of it all still sour on his tongue. Past a pawnbroker, a closed-up cafe, identikit branches of three rival burger chains pumping the same deep-fried shit into the early evening air; up and along the stretch of road leading up to the rapidly emptying shopping centre that looked ten times cleaner and better-kept than the city left to rot around it.

And stopped dead on the balls of his feet, less than two yards from the most beautiful woman he'd ever seen, her upper body – her head, shoulders, breasts – rising like mist from the pavement below.

She was naked: her pale white skin touched only by the blonde hair hanging long and loose to her waist and the leather strap that could've belonged to a soldier's musket bisecting her chest. And she was... not quite solid: the shape and detail of her seeming to solidify as she rose, obscuring the shops and the street and the straggling passers-by he was certain he could still see *through* her, if he focused.

But how was he *supposed* to focus, with a woman like that in front of him? How was anyone?

He watched, slack-jawed, as her ascent continued: her stomach, her belly button, then the smooth curve of her hips breaking the surface of the concrete; revealing themselves to him, inch by inch. She was... sitting down, or so he deduced from the angle of her spine. Was *perched* on something, a seat or a saddle.

Or a throne.

She saw him staring. Her bright blue eyes – half-closed before, her neck tilted backwards like she was taking in the sun, basking in the feel of it on her face – landed on his, and the look she gave him was so hot and intense it hurt his head and set his ears to ringing.

She nodded, as if she was answering a question he hadn't heard himself ask. Traced the fingers of one of her hands along her collarbone and pulled something he couldn't quite see – something thin and sharp and full of edges – from behind her back.

CHAPTER 9

SUNNY

It doesn't seem to Sunny so improbable that the spectral figure of the woman she presumes to be Godgifu – the Lady Godiva, late of Cofa's Tree – should be surging upwards from the laid-stone earth of the city: naked as a babe, her bare thighs clenched around the flanks of a spectral palfrey already beginning to steam about the withers. Few things, after all, are *entirely* improbable, when considered over tetraseconds and millennia.

Which isn't to say Sunny isn't surprised.

The Lady's countenance is stern, though as beguiling now in pellucidity as it must have been to Peeping Tom in its fleshly heyday. In her delicate left hand she grips a Norman sword, pungent with ozone and tinged – like Godiva herself and the horse she rode up on – a ghostly blue, but no less threatening for it.

The whetted tip of the sword hovers inches from the forehead of the definitely corporeal boy standing awestruck as a mooncalf before her: a hypertrophied pink gorilla of a thing, bunched at the neck but spindly at the jogging-bottomed legs, his underarms perspiring and knuckles, inexplicably, decanting drops of blood onto the ground at his feet.

His running shoes are dazzling white and perfectly cushioned; a heavenly counterpart to Bunny's infernal moccasins. Sunny notes their make and model; resolves to look them up online and perhaps even order herself a pair when all of *this* is passed.

Godiva's triceps flex, too quickly for the human eye to see, and Sunny knows at once what's coming; foresees the knight's sword cutting clean through the centre of the boy's head a second before it pierces the skin across the ridge of his brow.

He doesn't scream. Nor, to Sunny's further surprise, does he leak or haemorrhage from the wound, not even as the sword makes its inevitable departure through the rear of his skull. No fragments of bone splinter at the touch of the double-edged blade; no hot brain matter smears against its ethereal steel as it exits.

There is, in fact, no exit wound at all.

The boy's rabbit eyes widen, and Godiva flexes again, pulling the sword free of its quarry. He sways, punch-drunk; staggers this way and that, but doesn't fall. Just another daytime drunkard struggling to right his balance after one too many ales on an empty stomach, should anyone be watching.

Sunny doesn't believe anyone *is*, however. Just as she's confident that she and the boy are the only ones to register Godiva's presence: Sunny because her perceptions tend not to be restricted by such minutiae as visibility, and the boy – she must assume – because Godiva has willed it so. Has *chosen* him.

And, seeing him blink and clutch his wounded head and then lurch away, confused, from Godiva and her steed towards a painful death whose provenance he'll scarcely remember, when, minutes or hours from now, the moment comes... Sunny knows how this portion of the story will end.

If not yet, exactly, *why*.

Godiva disappears as swiftly as she rose, evaporating like a San Francisco flash fog into the grey surrounds of the city, and leaving Sunny alone with her suppositions.

Even the most third-rate of Poirots, she thinks, would bow at this juncture to the weight of evidence before them; would gather the suspects in the drawing room and denounce Godiva with a smug but irrefutable *J'Accuse*. What more could one deduce, having seen for themselves Godiva's assault on the boy's simian-thick cranium, *but* that the Lady was the cause of Anand Kumar's expiration? Of the lecherous Jonathan Foy's?

Clearly, incontestably, Godiva is the murderer: slayer of dentists, exploder of heads, scourge of Warwickshire's menfolk. What, though, is her motive? Wherefore this recent bloodbath? Mass murder is by and large a personal business, and ever has been: a game of vengeance and reprisal, of settling scores and remedying perceived slights. Or it's a calculation: the annihilation of pieces on a chaturanga board, for profit or advancement.

But Godiva, if Sunny is to believe the once-forgotten Domesday entries she calls now to mind, has been dead – buried, rotted and insensate – for some nine hundred years or more; too long by far to have *beef*, as Jonas might put it, with any living man in Cofa's Tree. With her own husband, perhaps; the Anglo-Saxon nobility had a reputation for cruelty that long outlived their dynasty. But with Kumar or

Foy, or this afternoon's barrel-chested child in his cheap athleisurewear?

Unlikely.

It's quite the puzzle. Quite the puzzle indeed.

———

She buys two warm but underdone elotes from a food cart vendor dressed as a buttered ear of corn. Finds a stone bench free of bird faeces, and sits, and eats, and ponders.

The purpose of her investigation has changed, and irrevocably. No longer is there a need to find *whodunnit*: who pulled the trigger and hid away the smoking gun; who slipped the digitalis in the crème de menthe as the guests played bridge.

Has the ascertaining of the *who*, though, ever *really* been the end-goal for a Poirot or a Marple, or even a Fiona, when the *why* and *how* have always proven so much more compelling?

Colonel Mustard stabbed the vicar with the baselard: this is nothing but a statement of fact, dry and dusty, of interest only to the sentencing judge. But the *why* of such a stabbing, the revelation that Colonel Mustard laid waste to the vicar after catching him with *Mrs* Mustard in the vestry... *That's* a story worth repeating. A story in which even Sunny might become invested.

The devil is in the details, yes – but so too is the delight.

CHAPTER 10

SUNNY

"There's a common thread here," Sunny muses aloud over another Vitellian breakfast banquet, this one combining the best of Nepalese and Oaxacan culinary traditions. "Something connecting these men, beyond their disposition towards women."

"Something other than Godiva's wrath, you mean?" says Bunny, drizzling a limp and uninspiring mole poblano over her Gorkhali toast.

It astonishes Sunny, still, that Bunny can have lived so long and seen so much, and yet have remained so infuriatingly obtuse. Though perhaps it was inevitable that Sunny's enumeration of her encounter with Godiva to one so unimaginative as Bunny, upon returning to the country pile the previous evening, would lead them here: to Bunny's confident dismissal of the case as closed, its mystery resolved.

"I'm speaking," Sunny replies, her patience spread as thin as the mole, "of Godiva's reason for targeting this particular cadre of gentlemen. Her *motivation*. It seems madness simply to assume she's been rising from the grave to dispatch them on a whim. There must be some stratagem at work here, some rationale for her... corporealizing thusly. One should proceed therefore, should one not, on the understanding that a more concrete commonality exists between our Cofa's Tree cadavers? And seek to understand the *victimology*, as I believe the criminologists would have it?"

"It's not like you to need a *reason* for a slaughter." Bunny's tone is mild, but Sunny cares not one bit for the insinuation, the moral superiority dripping like molasses from the words. "Perhaps you and Godiva are simply of one mind in that regard."

"Oh, there's always a reason, I assure you." Sunny spears a jeri swari from the communal bowl before her, sniffs delicately at its crispy edges, and – maintaining eye contact with Bunny all the while – returns it to the china platter whence it came, her unspoken verdict plain. "But I will concede, it takes a certain perspicacity to discern the pattern amid the disarray. A certain... savvy. You know?"

Bunny has an 11am brunch in Warwick with her Twelfth Night director, Terry – who must, Sunny assumes, be in want of more rewarding employment, to have agreed to such a date at such an hour. Unless Sunny is simply underestimating the scale of dedication a life in greasepaint demands of the amateur dramatist.

No matter: Sunny has a plan. The connection *will* be uncovered, the common thread unravelled. Her investigative spirit has been reinvigorated by the discovery of Godiva's involvement in this parochial bloodbath; she's certain, once again, that *she* will be the one to precipitate the unravelling.

Following the briefest of returns to Fiona's notes, and a briefer glance still – via Bunny's comically outdated desktop computer – at several of the more popular social media platforms, she flies, bepigeoned, to Leamington Spa, and from there to the two-bed Regency apartment of one Kimberley Dixon: the elder sister of Dean Weller, among the first of those whom Sunny has now mentally characterised as *Godiva's victims*. Weller's parents are based, she has discovered, in Nuneaton – a settlement which, while but a stone's throw away in geographic terms, once hosted a Priory of Benedictine nuns whose brief flirtation with occultism, and thereafter with demonic conjuration, cast something of a pall over Sunny's visits to the English counties in the latter decades of the fifteenth century. The memory still haunts her, and she has privately resolved to avoid it as assiduously as Betjeman avoided Slough. Kimberley Dixon and Leamington Spa, as a consequence, it must be.

Dixon, Sunny's desk research has informed her, is currently enjoying what the former's LinkedIn profile euphemistically terms *a career break*, taken – or possibly thrust upon her – following an eight-year stint as a specialist solicitor with the Proceeds of Crime Division of the Crown Prosecution Service. She is apt, like Naomi Foy, to be found at home, even on a weekday lunchtime. Thus, it is with no small amount of confidence that Sunny decants herself from her feathered form; strides, anthropoid and attired in illusory but inoffensive fabrics, to the front door of the property, and rings the bell for 11 Eliot Crescent, Flat 3.

In person, Dixon is much as her profile photograph has suggested: slim, brown-skinned (her genetic heritage, Sunny speculates, some admixture of Northern European and West African) and discreetly stylish in appearance, her hair cropped short and her heavy-rimmed eyeglasses bearing the just-visible mark of a Brazilian fashion designer for whom Jonas and his Innamorato profess an unhealthy devotion. She wears an emerald sarong tied loosely at the neck, a small stud of real diamond in each ear – and, most pressingly from Sunny's perspective, a look of curious suspicion quite in keeping with her former line of work.

"Can I help you?" she asks upon opening the door, with much the inflection Sunny, no stranger to the Law & Order franchise, imagines her weaponising in the courtroom as she faces down a gangland kingpin or a fallen smuggler of Egyptian antiquities.

"I'm from the coroner's office," Sunny begins, recalling a similar line deployed by the Chief Medical Examiner of the Special Victims Unit on visiting the home of a suspect in the company of Detectives Stabler and Benson.

"Yes?" Dixon's confusion deepens. "Which one?"

Such a follow-up question, Sunny did not anticipate. No matter.

"Leamington Spa," she answers, smooth and assured.

Dixon frowns, and then – to Sunny's surprise – releases a brief but hearty peal of laughter.

"That's not a thing." The woman grins, widely, a picture of amusement. "Come on: who are you, really?"

And Sunny resigns herself, again, to the deployment of the thrall.

"I know he was my brother," the now-thralled Dixon says from the kitchen sink, as she brews what smells to Sunny like a *very* acceptable ristretto, "but Dean was a bastard, an absolute bastard. To tell you the truth, I regret even going to the funeral. I thought at the time it was the right thing to do, for mum and dad, but now, looking back on it... I just don't know. You know?"

Sunny nods, sagely. "Absolutely."

"After all the shit he'd pulled, and I'm talking from *years* back, not just the recent stuff... Going there and mourning him, even just *looking* like I was mourning him – it's like, who am I kidding? *I'm* not sorry he's gone, so why should anyone else be?"

Her voice, not noticeably accented in the doorway, has roughened at the edges, lapsed into a regional colloquialism that speaks more of a childhood in the local area than an adulthood in London courtrooms. And she's loquacious, even by the standards of the thralled; positively confessional when contrasted with Naomi Foy.

Perhaps this is a topic she's needed to talk about for longer than these last few weeks. Perhaps a part of her has been waiting decades for someone – a stranger – to ask the necessary question.

"What kind of... stuff?" Sunny enquires.

Dixon sits down across from her at the table and hands her the ristretto, which is indeed exquisite: neither too bitter nor too weak. "Girls. It was always girls, ever since he was a kid. And not in a good way. I don't know if it was that he *liked* hurting them, that he got off on it, or that he just couldn't deal with people telling him no, turning him down... but it doesn't really matter which, does it? Either way, he *did* it. Makes no difference to those girls whether it was because mum and dad used to spoil him, or whether he was just a sadistic prick from the off."

Another Jonathan Foy, then, Sunny thinks. *Another Anand Kumar.*

Another man who hates women.

Godiva really does *have a type.*

"Were there ever... consequences?" she probes – slowly, carefully. "*Legal* ones, perhaps?"

Dixon laughs, but it's a very different laugh than her earlier display of amusement. *This* laugh is sour; it courses with melancholic bile. "You're not familiar with our sexual offences laws, I take it? Or the way the CPS works? Most complaints don't make it to court. And this is more anecdotal observation than professional opinion, but I'm telling you: most women don't even bother reporting, and I don't blame them. I'm not sure *I* would, in this climate."

Sunny thinks again of Jonathan Foy, and the receptionist at his practice. Of the rage, the utter loathing that suffused the *widow* Foy as she recounted their story.

You tell me, now: what would a good-looking fella like Johnny be doing sticking a camera up the skirt of a runty little thing like that?

"Indeed," Sunny murmurs.

"Mum and Dad knew," Dixon continues. "Or they were *told*, I should say. I'm ten years older than Dean, than Dean *was*, so I was already long gone when it started happening, and obviously they weren't going to talk to *me* about it when I was home, but some things you can't avoid hearing, can you? And not all the girls stayed quiet about it, even if they didn't press charges. Donna, my cousin... she said she was round at Mum and Dad's once when someone's granddad turned up on the doorstep with a machete, wanting to know where Dean was. They had to send him to stay with my uncle Stanley in Grenada until *that* one died down."

Sunny sips at her ristretto and ponders this information. It's essential background, of course – not to say confirmation of what she'd already suspected vis-à-vis victimology, if one considered such creatures as Foy, Kumar and Dean Weller *victims* of anything but preternatural justice dispensed. But she needs more: something more substantive tying Weller to Godiva in the here and now. And by extension, tying Godiva to her *other* human quarries.

"There was some mention," she says, "of *recent stuff*..."

Dixon removes her expensive eyeglasses; lays them on the table, and squeezes the bridge of her nose, remembering. "Yeah. I only know about *that* one because of his phone – Mum and Dad gave it to me after he died without even trying to unlock it. Stupid bastard hadn't bothered with a real password, anyway: *1234* was what he went with, if you can believe it. So I put it on charge, and I'm not going to lie, I had a look... and I saw his photos. What was *in* his photos – in his videos. *His* videos, you know? Not ones he'd been sent or ones he'd found somewhere online. Ones he'd taken himself."

"And...?" Sunny asks, when more than a moment of silence has passed.

"And the last video, the most recent one on there..." Dixon's voice falters. "I watched it. Watched the whole thing. Him and this girl, in his office." She closes her eyes, as if to exorcise the image. "That poor girl. That *poor* fucking girl."

CHAPTER 11

KIRAN

She was lying on her bed, trying to nap, when her mum called her downstairs. She checked her phone; saw it was 6.30, neither afternoon nor fully evening. A weird time for unexpected visitors to turn up on the doorstep, surely?

And it *was* a visitor waiting for her in the living room – her mum had been clear about *that*, even if the overloud and slightly slurred mode of her delivery as she'd shouted up the message from the hallway had made Kiran wonder, just for a second, if she'd been drinking. It wasn't like Harpreet to slip a whiskey in her coffee or knock back a glass or three of Pinot Noir while she cooked – she could barely be persuaded to accept a flute of Prosecco at a wedding, usually. But people were unpredictable, weren't they? You never really knew what they were capable of.

Kiran understood *that*.

Quietly, hoping her bare feet on the floorboards wouldn't betray her movements, she sloped across the landing to the bathroom. Splashed her forehead with cold water, ran a brush through her hair and slugged a capful of mouthwash, then – happy enough that neither chronic sleep deprivation nor her ever-present guilt and anxiety could be read in her face – trudged slowly and apprehensively down the stairs to meet whoever was insisting on seeing her.

Her first thought, on entering the living room, was that her mum really *was* drunk. Harpreet's eyes were unfocused, her posture so relaxed she might've just rolled off a masseuse's table, and the smile she threw Kiran as she rose from her recliner was dopey to the point of delirium.

"Here you are!" she said, ebullient as a game-show host. "We were just talking about you. I was telling your friend how proud me and your dad are of you – what a clever girl you are, and how lovely you've turned out. Isn't she lovely?"

The visitor, a youngish Middle Eastern-looking woman Kiran had never seen before in her life – dressed neck-to-calf in a criminally unflattering brown smock and, below the ankle, a pair of rose-gold trainers with luminous pink laces – nodded her agreement.

"Quite lovely, yes," the woman added, in a voice that seemed to Kiran legitimately devoid of accent, regional or otherwise. It wasn't a *posh* voice, per se; it wasn't honest-to-goodness RP or a regional dialect with the stuffing knocked out of it by elocution lessons. It just... wasn't *from* anywhere.

"Sorry, have we met?" Kiran asked her, not acknowledging her mum's uncharacteristic and frankly bizarre volley of maternal boasting.

The woman turned to Harpreet. "Would you mind?" She gestured to the door.

Harpreet, against all reason – and in defiance of every scrap of evidence Kiran had amassed in twenty-something years of knowing her mother – murmured what sounded like happy assent in response, then stood up from the recliner and trotted from the room, closing the door behind her.

Kiran stared at the stranger, open-mouthed and disbelieving.

"What is this?" she said, when she could speak again. "Who are you?"

"Not important." The stranger stretched back on the sofa and yawned – actually yawned, like a cat. "But it certainly *is* lovely to meet you. Your Human Resources person – Joanna, I believe? – was terribly complimentary about you when we spoke. *One of our most promising junior statisticians*: her words, not mine. And, of course, your mother was positively brimming with praise, as you heard."

Kiran's paranoia kicked in, hard. "You talked to Joanna? Why?" Another thought occurred to her. "Wait. Did she give you my address?"

"She did, she *did*," the stranger agreed happily, not just unfazed by the questions but apparently delighted that Kiran had made the deduction. Like Kiran was a guinea pig who'd performed a particularly complicated trick with an exercise ball and a piece of carrot. "An extremely accommodating woman, though perhaps – and this is only my opinion, of course – too prone to digression on the particular idiosyncrasies of the Bedlington Terrier. Are you aware of the breed? They're often mistaken for an ovine species at a distance, or so Joanna would have it, although I enquired into them myself on the *information superhighway*," she pronounced this slowly and carefully, as if describing a new cultural phenomenon with which Kiran might not yet be familiar, "and they seem to me undeniably canine in appearance. What sheep, after all, has an ear *that* shape?"

"What do you *want*?" Kiran said again.

"Straight to the point. I see." The stranger studied Kiran

– seeming to weigh her up, to get the measure of her. "I was hoping to ask you about Dean Weller. The *late* Dean Weller, I should say."

A cold spike of panic struck Kiran somewhere in the centre of her chest and radiated outwards to her limbs, her throat, her sinuses. Could she know? This woman, this stranger... could she have worked out what Kiran had done? The gist, anyway, if not the specifics – because no way in *hell* could anyone have guessed the *how* of it, only the *what* and (*please, no, anything but that*) the *why*.

"No," she said, as calmly as she could manage. "No, I don't think so. It was terrible, what happened to Dean, but I hardly knew him, except from work, so there's really nothing I can tell you that you won't know already. Whoever you are."

The stranger pursed her lips. Narrowed her eyes and tilted her head in a strange imitation of a sympathetic gesture that made her look, Kiran thought, like someone who'd had the appearance of empathy described to them, but who'd never had reason before that instant to put the theory into practice. "He really was a quite appalling crea-ture," she says. "I understand your resistance to discussing him. Unfortunately..."

"I'd like you to leave, if you don't mind," Kiran inter-rupted her. "Joanna shouldn't have told you my address, I'm not even sure that was *legal*, and you definitely shouldn't have turned up like this..."

But the instruction died away as it left her mouth, because the stranger was talking, too: harsh, guttural words in a language that definitely wasn't English or Spanish or Punjabi, almost certainly wasn't German or Hindi or Urdu or Polish, and sounded nothing like the Mandarin and Arabic Kiran had got used to hearing at work. It was *old*, though – she'd have sworn to that, though she couldn't have said why. Older than Sanskrit, older than Greek and Hebrew. And rhythmic: like hearing a song in Elamite or Ancient Sumerian crooned into a crackling microphone by a throaty French chanteuse.

"Perhaps I might stay after all?" the stranger concluded, in English this time. "And we might have... what's the appropriate colloquialism? A *quick chat*?"

Acute, blood-hot embarrassment flooded Kiran. More than embarrassment: shame. What had got *into* her, asking a guest to leave like that? What sort of person invited someone into their home and then turfed them out again, mid-conversation, without even offering to make them a coffee?

And the woman seemed so *nice*, too. So kind and understanding.

What was Kiran thinking, being so fucking *rude* to her?

"God, of course," she said quickly. "You stay sitting down, and I'll put the kettle on. Can I get you something to eat while you're there?"

"The two of you met at work?" the woman asked, once Kiran has made the tea and arranged a plate of Choco Leibniz on the coffee table in front of her. "You and Mr Weller?"

"Yeah," Kiran said. It was difficult even thinking about Dean, let alone *talking* about him... but the woman made it easier, somehow. Made it feel more like therapy than a confession. And, now she'd started, it was beginning to dawn on Kiran that, actually, she really *had* needed to talk to someone about this, after all. To drain away a bit of the poison she'd been storing up inside herself. "We were on the same graduate scheme. He wasn't brilliant at his job – I think he thought data analysis would be a bit more of a doss than it was – but he seemed like a nice bloke, and we starting hanging out a bit, at lunch and that. He used to bring me a salad at my desk when I had to work through. It was quite sweet, really."

"You were close?"

"Close? No, I wouldn't say that. He was definitely a *work person*, in my head – someone you'd see and get on with in the office, someone you'd have a laugh with, but not someone you'd *arrange* to meet up with, you know? And he was..." Kiran reddened. "He was quite fit. For a work person."

The woman's head tilt returned, this time signifying confusion. "He was an athlete?"

"No." Kiran worried the blush might swallow her whole. "Like... he was good looking, sort of."

"I see." The woman paused to finish her biscuit. "But things went downhill, I gather?"

Kiran's stomach tightened – but not enough, she realised, to stop the flow of words, to keep the stored-up toxins leaching out of her. "I guess." She picked up a sofa cushion; clutched it tightly to her body. "There was this one night we had to stay late, me and him, to get this presenta-tion done. Really late: like 9.30, 10 at night, and obviously there's nobody else there then but security, and they were all on the ground floor, so it really *was* only us. And we got done what we needed to, but by then we were both knack-ered, and starving hungry. So Dean got us a pizza delivered, and a few beers to celebrate that we'd managed to get every-thing sorted, and we stayed there drinking and talking for a bit, and it was all fine. And then... it wasn't."

She could pinpoint, afterwards, the exact moment she

realised he'd turned: that the jokey, matey approach he'd taken with up to that point had mutated into something more predatory, more threatening. They'd been sitting together until then, on the couch in the open-plan area, but there'd been a comfortable, collegial amount of distance between them, a gap big enough for another person to slide into. And then there hadn't been. Then Dean had been right next to her, his tree trunk thigh pressing into her hip and his arm snaking around her neck to take hold of her shoulder, and when she'd turned to ask him what he thought he was doing, the flat-eyed, basking shark grin he'd flashed back had scared the breath out of her.

She'd tried to push him off, but he'd pinned one of her wrists against the arm of the sofa, and the other above her head; manoeuvred his body on top of hers and between her legs. He'd been so heavy, but so quick with it, and the combination of the two had paralysed her. He'd pawed at her shirt, pulled off the buttons; torn open her bra. He'd been working at the zip of her trousers, losing patience with it, when she'd managed to get her left wrist free – and, with a burst of kinetic energy so forceful she wondered later where it had come from, had driven her forearm into the side of his neck and sent him sprawling to the floor on his arse.

She had, she'd known instinctively, all of about three seconds before he was back on his feet and on her again – this time wanting, most likely, to make her pay, make her hurt a bit for having humiliated him. So, she'd run, snatching her phone but not stopping to fix her bra or close up her shirt: run out of the office through the fire escape, down six flights of stairs and into the lobby; past the revolving doors, onto the mercifully busy street, and into the back of the first black cab that would stop for her.

And home.

"I called in sick the rest of that week," she told the stranger. "I didn't know if I'd go back at all, to be honest. But it was a really good job, and I didn't have anything else lined up, and how was I supposed to explain to everyone why I'd just *left*? I knew I wasn't going to tell anyone what actually *happened*. What he did. Nobody would've believed me. And you can imagine what people would've said: *what was she doing on her own with him that late, if she wasn't interested? Why was she* drinking *with him?*

"So... I know it sounds mental, I do, but the next week... I went back. Tapped in, sat back down at my desk and tried not to look over to where he was sitting.

"I managed to avoid him – more or less completely for the next fortnight, actually, which makes me wonder now if he was trying to avoid me too. I guess it'd make sense, if he was. *He* didn't know I wasn't going to tell anyone, did he? He might've been shitting bricks, thinking I'd go to HR and make a complaint about him. Or the *police*, even.

"I'd started applying for other stuff, other jobs. Even had an interview lined up. So, I just kept telling myself: stick it out a bit longer, and then it'll be over. Then you won't have to worry yourself sick about bumping into him at the canteen, or need to take yourself off to the bathroom with a stomach ache every time you see his name come up in your inbox or catch a look at the back of his head through the window of the conference room.

"And it nearly was, you know? It nearly *was* over." She dry-swallowed air. Wrung her hands together to stop them shaking. "But I didn't know what *else* he'd done, did I? What he'd been..."

The door swung open – *burst* open, really, like a heavy breeze had built up behind it – and suddenly Kiran's dad was in the living room with them, staring perplexedly at her and the stranger, his thick eyebrows knitting together in a hairy question mark.

Bal Nagra was neither a big man or an obviously astute one: he was too short, too scruffy, too poorly-put-together, his suit always slightly too tight or too baggy and the beard he insisted on keeping neither sleek enough to be fashionable nor long enough to be a statement of religious observance. In fact, he looked, as Kiran's friend Suki had once put it, *a bit ragged*: like he'd woken up too early, thrown on the first clothes he'd reached for in the dark and then left the house without so much as glancing in the mirror.

He *was* a lawyer, though. And he knew tension and a confessional atmosphere when he stumbled into the middle of it.

"Everything alright in here?" he said, squinting at Kiran, then at the stranger. "Kiran, love – who's your friend?"

Something in Kiran *shifted*, sharpening the edges of her thinking, her awareness of the room – like she'd downed a can of cold brew coffee, or was just starting to shake off a hangover. Because it was a very good question, wasn't it? Who *was* the woman? And why the *fuck* was Kiran spilling her guts to her about what happened with Dean that night in the office?

An even better question: why, *why*, was Kiran *about* to tell her what had happened with him afterwards?

She looked up at her dad, ready to tell him... *something* to explain away the obvious weirdness of the situation. But the stranger got there first.

"Oh, don't worry about *me*," she said, already darting for the open door, two of the biscuits dangling from her fingers. "I was... what's the phrase? *On my way out.*" She brushed past Bal, her oddly clothed body briefly insinuating itself against his as she made for the hallway. *Like a cat,* Kiran thought again; *just like a cat, rubbing up against you when it's trying to get outside.* Then, gracing Kiran with a *very* peculiar smile, she added: "It really *was* lovely to chat, though. *Most* informative. Perhaps we might catch up again soon?"

CHAPTER 12

SUNNY

The ruins of St Mary's Priory are cleaner, neater and less *ruined* by far than other abandoned ecumenical structures Sunny has known: the earthworks at Avebury, say, or the Megalithic Temples of Malta. New and healthier buildings, Victorian and younger, have been raised on the site of the former Priory, while protective glass and roped-off walkways conceptualise the ruins within – now excavated, tagged and labelled as meticulously as any paleontological find at Lake Mungo or the caves of Sterkfontein – not as a monument to the anti-papal extirpations of a Tudor king, but as conceptual *pieces*: a deconstructed art-in-stone.

This framing, Sunny imagines, plays better for the tourists than a mound of mottled masonry alone, even one steeped in five-hundred-year-old zealotry.

There are, however, no tourists here this late in the evening. Nor are there tour guides, enthusiastic in their chaperons and period breeches. Tonight, there is only Sunny, and the girl she has pursued here, *tailed* here from the residential enclaves of the former Cofa's Tree: a girl from whom the isothermal whiff of borrowed magic emanates so strongly it's a wonder no friend or passer-by has choked on it.

Sunny had known she was at the heart of the Godiva situation from the moment she'd laid eyes on the girl, long before the father's unfortunate interruption. The *why* is more apparent than ever to her now. Who *wouldn't* seek to peel the wastrel flesh from Dean Weller's curdling bones, in the girl's position? And the connection, that elusive thread linking each man Godiva has targeted to the other... that too is becoming clearer to Sunny, in the wake of the detection she's performed that day. Detection of which she is, if she says so herself, inordinately proud.

The exact *how* remains unanswered, as yet. But it seems to Sunny, as she watches the girl pick an unsteady path across the sanitised ruins towards the spot under which Godiva lies buried, that this too will be made manifest, and soon.

Upon arriving at the spot in question, the girl pauses. She reaches into the olive-green knapsack strapped about her person, and retrieves from within it a book, large and old and apparently leather-bound. It is, if not the *exact* tome Sunny had anticipated, then certainly in the vicinity thereof, thaumaturgically speaking.

(The binding, of course, is *not* leather. It is, rather, a Frankensteinian amalgam of cured skins, both human and demoniacal: some as ancient as the book's appearance suggests, and others... less so. Sunny decides, on the whole, that omitting mention of this particular detail might be prudent, if the girl's trust is to be won, and the puzzle solved thereafter).

"Hello again," she says, slipping from the shadows and allowing herself to be seen.

Startled, the girl loses her grip on the book, which falls

to the once-hallowed earth with a portentous thud.

"What are you doing here?" she asks Sunny, a burst of righteous anger only thinly veiling her alarm. "Have you been following me?"

"Godgifu, Lady Mercia," Sunny answers her, deliberately elliptical. "*Lady Godiva*, as you no doubt know her. I was hoping you might tell me how you persuaded her to lay waste to Dean Weller and his bedfellows?" She makes a show of surveying the girl, examining her, from the fragility of her stature to the frightened tremor that vibrates along her lower lip. "You're rather an unlikely necromancer."

Though perhaps, she qualifies, for her own benefit if not the girl's, *no more unlikely than Jonas might have seemed, this time last year, with his boyband hair and white-toothed smile.*

The girl shakes – actually *shudders* – at the accusation.

"I'm not a..." She stalls, as if unable even to give voice to the word. "It shouldn't have happened. Any of it. I didn't mean it to."

"You didn't intend to harm Mr Weller?" If true, this sentiment surprises Sunny. In the girl's stead, were physical retribution an option for one such as her, she would have *revelled* in reducing his grey matter to a neuroglial pulp.

"No! Or, I don't know..." Again, the girl falters. "I don't know *what* I wanted. To get back at Dean, maybe. Make him hurt, or something. But not *kill* him, I never wanted that. And as for the others..."

"The others?" Sunny feels she must clarify this point. Are there more of the slaughtered out there than even she or Fiona or the science fiction-reading Coroner are aware? "Mr Foy, and Mr Kumar, and that young solicitor – I'm afraid his name escapes me? And..."

The girl winces, but is apparently not so pained by the recounting of the fallen as to be prevented from interrupting

Sunny mid-flow. "Yeah. Them. All of them. But I didn't mean it, you know? I swear to you I didn't. I didn't know them. I hadn't even *heard* of them, until..."

As confessions go, this is less satisfying than the rage-soaked antagonist's soliloquy Sunny might have had hoped for. There is no Jacobean villain concealing itself in the dark heart of *this* Act of the tragedy, she suspects; only a frightened child with a guilty conscience, so desperate to unburden herself that she'll relinquish every last detail of her crimes upon the gentlest of probing.

Nevertheless, there *is* something else here too, some darker depth still to plumb; Sunny senses it. And there is, of course, the question of how the child came to have in her possession a volume as powerful as the one she carries with her currently – and how she acquired the necessary knowledge to put it to its intended use.

Though perhaps these answers too will reveal themselves, in the fullness of time.

"Until?" she prompts the girl.

A histrionic crack of thunder, entirely unheralded by the hitherto warm and cloudless night, unleashes itself across the heavens. Sunny rolls her eyes. If the universe has a sense of humour, she suspects, then it tends towards the slapstick – towards Vaudevillian volleys of banana-skin absurdity, the celestial equivalent of a phallus and a pair of dangling testes scrawled in marker pen across the bathroom door of the cosmos.

And now the girl is crying.

"I would've let it go," she says, through tears illuminated by an overwrought sky. "Even with what Dean did, I *would've*. But then I found out about the video, didn't I? The video, and that... group he was in. And after that... I had to do *something*. I had to."

CHAPTER 13

KIRAN

She was reluctant to drink, after The Thing with Dean. Didn't go clubbing or out to the pub; didn't go *anywhere*, really. Just to work, and once a week to practice with the arts group she'd signed up to a few months before, almost all of whom were gentle old hippies twice or three times her age, too unthreatening to set off any fight-or-flight reactions. It felt safer to stay in, locked in her room, reading and sketching and listening to music so loud it almost, though never quite drowned out the thoughts she was running from.

Then, when a handful of weeks had passed, she was confronted with a social event she couldn't avoid or lie her way out of with a sudden-onset stomach bug. A birthday party: her *best friend*'s birthday party, no less, and one for which Kiran had been given almost a year's worth of advance notice.

Erin lived in London these days: had moved there almost immediately after she and Kiran finished at Warwick, taking up a postgrad study placement at a cult film library near Brent Cross and a box room in a house-share in Hendon that backed on to a motorway and smelled like cat litter, but that cost her a grand a month in rent regardless, bills excluded. The distance meant Kiran hadn't had to see her in person in the aftermath of The Thing, or look at her, or have *her* look at Kiran, but had been able instead to deflect Erin's many, many questions – about work, and their other friends, and any new guys Kiran might be into – over text and email, parrying each new line of enquiry with a well-placed GIF or a thumbs-up emoji.

But Erin loved birthdays, and especially loved a birthday-adjacent event. Which was why, Kiran presumed, she'd decided to go all-out for her 25th: to book a venue, pick a theme ("Mermaids & Crustaceans: No Costume, No Entry"), invite what seemed like everyone they'd known at uni... and do it all in Coventry, "where adulthood began!"

There was no getting out of it. No excuse believable enough, no incapacitation severe enough to justify Kiran not attending a party her best friend had organised *in Kiran's hometown* and around which Kiran had had ample time to rework her schedule, should any reworking have proved necessary.

And so, dampening down the low-key panic that seemed to grip her whenever she'd left the house since The Thing, even – and sometimes especially – when it was only to walk a mile down the road to the office, she'd put on the most conservative halter top-and-mermaid tail combination she'd been able to find online, ordered a cab to Earlsdon and presented herself, neither awkwardly early nor fashionably late, at the rooftop bar Erin had hired to mark the occasion.

It was busy. Obviously, it was busy: it was *Erin*, who loved everybody and who everybody loved, and who could always be relied on to liven up a gathering with a Dolly Parton remix and a novelty cocktail. If she hadn't been so lovely, so genuinely kind – or so it had occurred to Kiran more than once since fate had thrown them together as freshers at a Theatre Society social – then Kiran would probably have hated her.

The happy upside of this busyness, and of Erin's preoccupation with meeting-and-greeting guests as they arrived, was the opportunity it afforded Kiran to hide away: to skulk around in the darker corners of the bar, the lemonade and lime-slice in her glass masquerading as a gin and tonic, dodging old friends and total strangers at the bar and shutting down any conversational gambits from which she couldn't physically extricate herself by staring, very pointedly, at her phone.

Until the fifth lemonade kicked in, and she found herself needing the bathroom.

Bathrooms were a danger zone at parties; Kiran had been cornered often enough at the sinks by sobbing drunks and saucer-eyed girls who'd downed one bomb of MDMA too many to be wary of the obstacles they placed in the path of the socially disinclined. This one, though, was empty, her door-to-stall trajectory mercifully clear. Her relief was almost overwhelming.

She entered the stall; peed. Checked her phone and readjusted her tail.

Opened the door and saw that someone else had entered the bathroom. Another girl from uni, though one who'd always been far better friends with Erin than with Kiran: a Scouser from Erin's English Lit course, one who'd hung around the area after graduating instead of going back home. Danielle... something.

She'd positioned herself by the hand-dryers, her back against the wall. Her makeup was smudged, her lower lip trembling and her body shaking inside a costume that seemed to be 90% seashells and shellac. And of course, she was crying.

The sound of the stall door opening and closing caught her attention, and she looked up. Locked eyes with Kiran and froze, as if she'd seen a ghost.

"Sorry," Kiran said, because what else were you supposed to say when you burst in on someone crying, even if they *were* doing it in what was technically a public place? Danielle didn't reply, though – just stood there *gawping* at Kiran and gaping like a fish. "Are you alright?" Kiran added, after an awkward few seconds. "Can I get you anything?"

It took a few seconds more for the words to land, for Danielle to react. Then came the laughter, loud and manic: a jagged saw-screech of hysteria that vibrated unhappily along the nerves of Kiran's teeth.

"No." She let loose another mad cackle. "No, I'm not fucking *alright*, actually."

Fair enough, Kiran thought. *I'll fuck off, then, shall I?*

"Right," she said aloud. "Okay. I'll just…"

She headed for the main exit; for the noise and heat of the party that lay behind it.

Danielle caught her by the arm as she was turning the handle.

"Wait." She rubbed her cheeks with the finger of a scale-covered glove and made a stab at an apologetic smile. It wasn't a wild success, but Kiran appreciated the effort regardless. "I'm sorry, I'm being a dick. It's just… It's been a bit of a rough night, you know what I mean?"

"Yeah." Kiran tried to return the smile, but managed only a small, painful upward movement of the muscles in her cheeks and lips that she suspected made her look like The Grinch on his way to steal Christmas.

"I just broke up with someone," Danielle added. "Day

before yesterday."

"Ah," Kiran said. She could hear the PA system cranking up outside, strains of '90s dance seeping in through the cracks in the door – if not quite calling to her, then certainly suggesting that the frying pan might be a bit more comfortable, in the immediate term, than the fire in which she was currently roasting.

"I didn't think he was like that." Danielle lowered herself onto the sink until her legs dangled from the basin, not quite touching the floor. *She's settling in*, Kiran realised, with no small amount of panic. *She's got a story to tell, and* someone's *going to fucking hear it.* "I thought he was solid, like. Someone you wouldn't mind meeting your mum. Not someone who'd..."

"Who'd what?" Kiran asked, before she could stop herself.

Danielle hesitated. Looked Kiran dead in the eye, like she was weighing something up, trying to come to some sort of decision. "Someone who'd treat women like that," she said. "Someone who'd talk about them with his mates like they were whores and sluts. Like all of them were asking for it."

It was a horrible story, and triggering, but Kiran kept listening anyway. Maybe *because* it was so horrible. *Because* it was so triggering. There was something darkly cathartic about hearing about it second-hand; having the awfulness of it filtered through the prism of someone else's disgust.

Stu, until very recently Danielle's boyfriend, had been acting oddly, she said: distant and distracted, never really listening when she spoke, and always on his phone. Since this marked a change from the attentive and *present* face he'd shown her in the previous six months they'd been together, Danielle started to suspect – not unreasonably, Kiran considered – that he was cheating on her. That he'd met someone else, at the gym or the restaurant where he worked, and was thinking about her, *texting* her even when he was curled up on the sofa watching TV with Danielle.

Which was why, the morning of the Thursday before they were due to go together to Erin's party – Danielle as The Little Mermaid, Stu as Sebastian the crab – she'd snatched his phone from the nightstand by her bed while he was in the shower and, using the passcode she'd seen him tap into it a hundred times before, began to trawl systematically through his messages.

There were none in his inbox from any woman but Danielle herself: nothing from female friends or work colleagues, not a whisper from any aunties or cousins. And probably, she thought afterwards, that was a red flag in itself.

What there *was*, was a very active group message thread, right at the top of the inbox: hundreds and hundreds of texts – and images, and videos – exchanged what seemed like every few minutes between Stu and a group of men calling themselves the Cov City Fuckboys.

"It was disgusting, all of it," she told Kiran. "Not just, like, your usual lad banter – it was really, really nasty shit. Stuff about random women, mostly – calling them *whores* and *sluts*, saying what they'd do to some of them, and that some other ones were too ugly to bother raping. All that Andrew Tate bollocks. You know the sort of thing."

Kiran did, of course. But she felt sick to her stomach anyway at the mention of it.

"I shouldn't have looked at the videos," Danielle said. "I

mean, I *know* I shouldn't have, because I knew before I looked what I was going to see, sort of. That it wouldn't be good, you get me? And it wasn't, was it? It just... wasn't."

She closed her eyes and leaned back over the sink, her head against the fingerprint-smeared mirror.

"I'm sorry." And Kiran *was*, she really was: sorry for Danielle, and sorry for whoever was in those videos. Sorry for herself, too.

"I must've watched about ten of them before I chucked the phone away." Danielle's voice was closer to a whisper as she spoke now, her tone recasting the women's bathroom as a therapist's couch. "Not all the same stuff, but all the same *type* of stuff, if you get me? People shoving their cameras up girls' skirts when they didn't know they were being filmed; girls giving blowjobs and blokes recording it from above, and the girls not realising they were being recorded. Just gross, horrible stuff. And the idea of Stu looking at it, him *talking* about it with those sickos in that group chat..." She shivered; ran her hands up and down her bare arms like she was warming herself. "Then I started worrying about what *Stu* might've shared. Whether there were any videos of *me* on that thread, and whether he'd been filming *me* for those sick fuckers to wank over. So, I picked the phone back up and took it downstairs, and I went through all the videos, every one of them, to make sure. And then he came downstairs, dressed and out the shower, and he saw what I was doing, and the *look* on his face... like he knew he'd been caught, and he knew the axe was about to fall. Knew that was it finished, that we were over. I mean, he must've done, mustn't he? 'Cause he didn't try to lie about it or explain it away. Didn't beg for forgiveness or any of that shite, either. Just said he was sorry, took his phone out my hand and walked out the door."

Outside, someone turned up the volume of the PA system, and the music thickened, its bassline driving up through Kiran's sinuses like a second pulse. There was static in her ears; something heavy pressing, hard and harder, on her lungs.

She'd never had a panic attack before. Had no personal point of reference to work out whether what she was feeling fit the bill, or whether she really *was* dying, after all. Either way, a vital part of her was shutting down, even as Danielle was speaking: sucking away her breath and digging cold, sharp fingers into her chest.

She had to get out.

"Sorry," she said, again. And then, like Stu, she walked away.

"Kiran."

She hadn't expected Danielle to find her later. Hadn't really, if she was honest with herself, expected Danielle to talk to or even acknowledge her again, after Kiran ditched her in the bathroom.

But Danielle *had* found her, and deliberately: tracking Kiran down outside the venue while she waited for her taxi and sitting down next to her on the kerb, seashells rattling with every movement of her arms.

"I owe you an apology," she said.

"What? No." Kiran had been too embarrassed to even look at her, though she could feel her own cheek burning from the intensity of Danielle's stare. "*I* should apologise. I didn't mean to just, like... run off. I've just... I've had some stuff going on. You know?"

She could feel Danielle nodding, somewhere in her

peripheral vision.

They sat together in silence for longer than was comfortable, Kiran's phone tracking the progress of the taxi as it crossed the city to get to her. 10 minutes away. 9 minutes. 8.

"I need to ask you something," Danielle said eventually. "And I don't really know how to say it, so I'm just gonna ask, okay?"

"Okay."

Danielle fished a vape pen from her bag and took a long, slow drag of something sweet and cherry scented. "Do you know someone called Dean? Dean Weller?"

The white noise rushed back in, flooding Kiran's ears, seeming to carry along her cheekbones and down, to the back of her throat. The fingers that had begun to loosen tightened in her chest, squeezing and choking, and her eyes watered, blurring the streetlights above her to a sodium haze.

"Yes," she said.

She didn't ask why. Even then, a part of her didn't need to.

"Right." Another drag on the vape, followed by another cloud of pseudo-smoke, engulfing Danielle's face. "So, here's the thing. I'm not sure I should be telling you this, but I think you've got a right to know, you know what I mean? Like, *I'd* want to know."

Say it, Kiran thought. *Just fucking say it.*

"This Dean." Kiran could *hear* her swallowing; *hear* the struggle to get the words out. "He was one of the people Stu had been messaging. One of the dickheads in the group chat. And the thing is... I looked through all the videos, right? With all the girls in them. And *Stu* didn't share any, that I saw. But that Dean did. And I'm sorry, K, I'm so fucking sorry, but I think you were in one of them."

CHAPTER 14

SUNNY

The girl clutches at the flesh-bound book – as if, Sunny thinks with a dry inner smile, it might protect her from evil. As if its power lies in warding, and not in the summoning of things against which warding may prove necessary.

"You know what's funny?" she says.

"No," Sunny answers, honestly. The comedic instincts of humans have never entirely gelled with her own.

The girl, fortuitously, seems to take her response as nothing more than a polite phatic: an injunction to speak further, to bare yet more of her soul.

"What's funny," she continues, the punchline reiterated, apparently for emphasis, "is that I did almost exactly what Danielle did. I waited 'til we were both back at work on Monday, then I took Dean's mobile off his desk while he was off getting coffee – and I went through his messages. Through his videos. His group chats."

Sunny thinks of Kimberley Dixon, breaking into her dead brother's telephone with the ease of an international jewel thief palming cubic zirconia earrings from an Argos counter. Of the complacency, the low-level hubris of Weller himself: a man so thoroughly convinced no ill would ever befall him, despite his own predations, that he barely saw fit to use passwords, neglecting even the most basic of security protocols.

Of how little of value has been lost, with Weller's passing.

"He'd filmed it. What he did to me." The girl squeezes the book: less a talisman now than a stuffed bear, held tight for comfort. "Rested his phone somewhere so it was pointed at us, and set it to record, while he..."

Had Miranda been alive to hear of this a month before, Sunny thinks, she would have skinned Weller's hide and hung what remained from the branches of an oak before Godiva could rise from the earth. For all her faults, and even Sunny will concede they were many, the woman had an admirable knack for a well-done flaying.

"Thing was, he hadn't *just* filmed it," the girl continues. "He'd edited it. Made it look like I, you know... was *into* it. Then he'd shared it. Sent it onto all those... those *bastards* in his group."

"I see." And for Sunny, the penultimate puzzle-piece slides into its place. "And one of *those bastards* would be, if I may venture a guess, Jonathan Foy? And Anand Kumar another?"

The girl sighs. "And Richard Hill, and Stuart Prescott – Danielle's ex. All of them. All the Cov City Fuckboys. Twelve altogether, plus Dean."

"How appallingly New Testament." Sunny wonders how many of the thirteen remain, if any, but thinks better of voicing any such speculation. The girl already has the look, as Jonas might put it, of a woman on the edge. There's no sense at all in pushing her further still towards the precipice.

"I don't think they knew each other. Offline, anyway," the girl adds, before Sunny can leap in with any such follow-up query. "The way they were talking, it didn't seem like they'd, you know, met up in person or anything. And Danielle didn't think so, either. She said none of the names were ones she recognised, or people she'd heard Stu mention. Doesn't make it any better, obviously, but... still."

Still *indeed*, Sunny concludes. *Still, they weren't hunting together in packs, out in the world. Still, it was videos they were sharing: just videos, and not the actual bodies of any mutual victims.*

Still. Such a multitude of sins, contained within so very slight a word.

"Brought together by a common interest, one presumes," she says aloud. "And it was this list of names, then, that you took to Godiva, once the grimoire came to be in your possession? That book you're holding," she clarifies, in response to the girl's blank stare, her obvious incomprehension.

Cut her some slack, she can almost hear Jonas whisper in her ear – chastising Sunny, as ever, for what he perceives as pathological fault-finding on her part, her predisposition towards the censorious. *Not everyone can recite the Testament of Solomon backwards, you know.*

"Yes," the girl confesses, sounding small and ashamed. "I just... I had to do something, you know? I couldn't just let him do that and get away with it. I had to do *something*."

And now it's *Miranda's* voice that Sunny hears, speaking not to Sunny but to another woman, in another time and place: Miranda framed by the glass walls of a summer-house-turned-abattoir, a bloody knife between her gloved digits and a butcher's row of hollowed-out corpses before her. *We couldn't just let them carry on hurting us, could we?*

"I didn't mean for it to happen," the girl adds quickly.

"Not to the others, anyway. It was only Dean I wanted to, you know..."

"Hurt?" Sunny doesn't give her the chance to respond. Other questions remain here, and larger. "There are two points with which I struggle, however. Or two points, perhaps, upon which the tendrils of my understanding come unspooled. Namely: how, precisely, did you happen upon that grimoire of which we spoke? And how, perhaps more pertinently still, were you able to interpret its instructions?" She pauses. Allows the girl to process what she's asking. "That is: through what means did you acquire the requisite knowledge to put it to use in the service of raising Godiva from the soil, so that she might seek vengeance in your name? I'm not, as it so happens, entirely unfamiliar with the contents of the text, nor with the language in which it's written. And while it's *possible* I've misjudged your capabilities, and gravely, it seems to me unlikely that you learned the necessary Old East Slavic at your mother's knee."

Softly, the girl replies. So softly, in fact, that Sunny must beg her to repeat herself.

"I saw it on TikTok," she says, only a little less faintly.

And so falls into place the very final jigsaw piece.

Really, ought Sunny not have to foreseen this – or at the very least, to have considered the possibility? *She*, after all, is no stranger to TikTok, not to any of its sister-platforms. Not since Jonas thrust upon her his tiny tablet computer and its perpetual loop of culinary preparation and performance. She is well aware, moreover, that there exists a world of *content* therein that extends beyond the realms of the merely gastronomic: videos showcasing the physiognomy of unusually unattractive cats, for example. Videos of soothsayers and those purporting to divine the future from the stars, confined no longer to the mountains or the madhouse but broadcasting live from occultly decorated living rooms in Albuquerque and São Paulo. Videos of faith healers and magicians, casting prayers and non-specific wellness out to every corner of the universe in exchange for a monthly stipend so small you'd barely notice it had left your bank account.

Of *course* there would be necromancy there, too. Of course there would be instructions on the uses of the darkest and most ancient of the Arts, in this world where even the most respectable and middle-class of English witches coordinate their sabbats over SMS.

"Go on," Sunny urges the girl.

"It was after I saw all that stuff on his phone. Saw the video. The people he'd sent it to." The girl rubs at her reddening eyes with the index finger of one hand - though she continues, Sunny observes, to cling to the grimoire as if her life depended on it. "I didn't know what to do. I talked to a friend about it – not Erin, no-one actually connected to any of it – and she was nice, and she said all the right things, but it didn't really help, you know? It didn't tell me what I was supposed to *do*. And it wasn't like I could've confronted Dean about it and told him to take down the video, was it? He would've laughed in my face. Probably taken a picture of me crying and sent *that* on to his mates as well."

Yes, Sunny thinks. *Yes, probably he would have.* Casual cruelty is red meat to men of Weller's persuasion. She's seen as much for herself, all too many times.

"So, I started looking around online for something useful. Something that wasn't just... sympathy. And then..."

The girl's red eyes grow dim. Lost in remembrance, perhaps? Ordinarily Sunny might be inclined to believe so. But there's something more *here*, too, something Sunny can't yet name; something that defies identifiable form, but of which she catches the faintest scent nevertheless, just as she did the ethereal contrails of the girl's borrowed magic.

"Tell me what you found there," she says – not in English but in the old tongue, the mother tongue. That which compels; which cannot be denied. "Tell me how you learned of the grimoire, and who gave it to you."

"I don't remember," the girl answers. There's a robotic quality to her rejoinder. A hint, if Sunny isn't mistaken, of something akin to post-hypnotic suggestion.

Fascinating. What *have* these TikTok necromancers been up to? What reservoir of power have they stumbled upon, that not only confers immunity to the old tongue but allows for its transmission to others over time and distance?

What *exactly* has been implanted into this girl's memory – or, worse yet, removed therefrom?

"Tell me." Sunny allows a chthonic timbre to permeate this second request. Not enough to harm the girl – as if she *could*, even if she wanted to; as if harming the girl, or any such human, were a possibility. But enough, perhaps, to scramble past whatever digital enchantments have been overlaid upon the girl's mind.

"I don't remember," the girl repeats – the intonation now not entirely *hers*, but imbued with unearthly harmonics that remind Sunny, quite unexpectedly, of the protagonist of an ostensibly *classic* moving picture Dan and Jonas – knowing grins splitting apart their cherubic man-child faces – insisted Sunny watch with them, the previous All Hallows' Eve. Of a fictional child, possessed by a demon of unspecified origin, screaming profanities at a priest from her sickbed – an inauthentic premise if ever Sunny heard one, given the reluctance of those demons *she* knows to spend even a moment in the company of children.

Your mother sucks cocks in hell, indeed.

Really, though: this *is* fascinating.

"Tell me," she demands of the girl, or whatever has taken hold of her.

A thin milky film, a kind of cataract, descends over the girl's eyes. "I. Don't. Remember," she, or whomsoever has her spellbound, insists.

And this, Sunny understands, is as much of an answer as she's likely to get to this particular question, no matter how hard or how often she pushes.

She really *must* look into those TikTok necromancers. Whoever they are.

"My apologies." She changes tack – what choice has she? – and the girl's eyes clear. She blinks. Focuses on Sunny.

"I want it to stop," she says, a note of pleading injected into what is obviously a statement of fact. This girl has no appetite for bloodshed; whatever vengeance she's set in motion, it's left the bitterest of residues. "I just want it to stop."

"I understand," Sunny tells her, though this *is* a lie: she herself can only savour the sweetness of these particular deaths.

But then, perhaps even the best of things must come to an end, eventually. And perhaps it *wouldn't* do to have an Anglo-Saxon noblewoman raring around the countryside on spectral horseback, exploding brain stems willy-nilly.

Miranda, of course, would have welcomed the prospect; might even have lent Godiva her assistance, were any required. Jonas, though, is another matter. The boy has *ethics* – a conscience sharp and unyielding as an arrow.

What would *he* say, if he knew? How would *he* react to Sunny's... failure to intervene?

He wouldn't allow her a moment's peace: this much she knows. Not until she swore to *put things right*.

So utterly, utterly insufferable, that boy.

She sighs, loud enough to wake the dead, and capitulates to the inevitable. "Give me the book," she says, stretching a hand out to the girl. "And we'll see what can be done."

CHAPTER 15

SUNNY

At Sunny's urging, and with no small amount of relief, the girl flees the sterile necropolis, her anxieties quelled.

The situation will be resolved, Sunny has assured her. Godiva will be placated, her killing spree brought to a close. Sunny will make certain of it.

The girl was happy to be convinced.

Alone among the buried dead, Sunny considers her options. Summoning Godiva ought to be – as the amateur bakers so often put it, with a knowing wink to the camera – *a piece of cake*; no Slavic grimoire required, though Sunny is pleased to have wrenched the one she holds now from the girl's grasp. Few weapons should be wielded by hobbyists, no matter how righteous their cause.

There remains, however, the question of what to *say* to Godiva, on having summoned her.

Neither divine law nor infernal injunction prevents Sunny doing harm to the dead: only to the living and the human. But nor has she any power over them to speak of, beyond the capacity to summon them before her. All she has, in fact, are empty threats.

If Godiva is to be stopped, therefore – Sunny must *persuade* her to stop. Must *negotiate* with her.

And diplomacy has never been Sunny's strongest suit.

But then: what can she do but press on, now she's come this far? Would Poirot retreat, having fallen so deep into the rabbit hole? Would *Jessica Fletcher*?

Perhaps the way forward is clear, after all. And doubtless she will think of *some* assuasive case to lay before Godiva, when the time comes.

She lets the words fall from her lips to the soil, and Godiva rises anew, naked and ethereal, now *sans* horse but translucent still, her knight's sword holstered at one handsome hip.

When even the soles of her bare feet have broken free of their tomb, she takes in her immediate surrounds: the Priory, the ruins, her audience.

"You're new," she says, the Germanic lift and fall of her Old English landing somewhere between post-Roman Jutland and ABBA Gold. "What's become of the girl?"

"Gone." Sunny stares out at Godiva, eye to ghostly eye. "It was she who woke you? Originally, I mean?"

Godiva snorts, mocking but nonetheless genteel. "*Originally*? No, certainly not. Most recently, perhaps. But she's not the first to have sought my relief, and she shall not be the last."

Sunny looks down at the undisturbed earth, and wonders: how many other victimised women have there been? How many more have called for Godiva and her blessing over the centuries, pain and anger boiling inside them and an alien incantation rolling from their tongues?

"Commendable," she says. "Your chamber must be quite awash with thank you cards."

Godiva's delicate features crinkle in suspicion. "And who

are you? You are no supplicant. Only humans come to beg my favour."

Sunny shrugs, an exaggerated *you got me* gesture. And, since there seems no reason now to persist in her current form, she allows herself to change, to become again the most instinctive – or perhaps simply the most comfortable – version of herself: willing horns to branch up and out from the flesh of her forehead; toes to fuse and harden into hooves, and skin to morph from brown to blue. "I hadn't intended to beg," she replies. "Only to request that you... dial down the androcide. In this one instance."

"I fear not your frightful visage, daemon." There's defiance in Godiva's stance now, if not outright contempt.

Sunny, meanwhile, is positively affronted. "*Frightful*? Come now, Godgifu. You must surely have seen worse than *this* in whichever nether realm has lent you quarter, this last millennia. Besides which, I'm not *asking* that you fear me. Simply, as I said, that you put an end to this latest... commission. The girl Kiran is satisfied. Justice is served. Sigh no more, ladies – sigh no more. And so on."

"Justice? As *if*," Godiva says, dipping briefly out of 11th century Mercian and into late-20th century Valley Girl. "No lady shall ever know *true* justice, not in this world of men."

I see someone *has issues*, Sunny thinks – Jonas' voice of conscience, of reason, momentarily supplanted by the generically waspish tones of a television network drag queen.

Pettish or not, though, the point has merit. Godiva pulses with choler, her allusions to the *world of men* around her laced with what seems to Sunny very personal grievances. Might this be something for Sunny to leverage, in the spirit of diplomatic persuasion and the building of trust?

Something over which they might *bond*, immortal to immortal?

Certainly, there are many men whom Sunny has wished dead – nay, whose deaths she has helped facilitate, albeit at a necessary distance. Perhaps Godiva might *relate*, in the pop-therapeutic parlance of the present, to the instinct that precipitated these kills?

It's surely worth a try.

"Quite right," she agrees, nodding energetically. "This is a man's world, is it not? But I tell you now, Godgifu: it would be nothing, *nothing* without a woman. Or a girl."

Godiva returns the nod. They are simpatico.

"All we're asking for," Sunny continues, warming to her theme even as she plunders her internal back-catalogue of contemporary self-empowerment anthems, "is a little respect. Because *they don't own us*, Godgifu. They can't tell us what to do, and they can't tell us what to say."

"Some have tried." Godiva licks her lips, and smiles at the memory – reminiscing, Sunny presumes, on some of the more satisfying of her past executions.

"Doubtless, they had it coming. They only had themselves to blame."

"I always hoped to kill my husband," Godiva says. Sunny's ears prick up at this disclosure, even as Godiva's smile recedes. "It is the greatest of my sorrows, that the fever took him first."

And that, Sunny thinks, *is exactly the nature of ghosts. Never quite able to let go of the past. Forever hanging on to those old grudges.*

"This would be Leofric?" she asks. "Earl of Mercia, favourite of Cnut The Great?" Then, because the odds are good, given the mores of the man's place and era, she adds: "Rather an unpleasant character, as I heard it."

Godiva brushes phantasmal fingers against the hilt of her sword. "Do you know why I bring my horse to the hunt?" she says after a moment. "Why I take to his saddle in pursuit of those I stalk?"

Honestly: no, Sunny does not. What one might call the *aesthetics* of spectral apparitions have always remained for her something of a mystery.

The morphic fields of the after-living – their physical appearance, their demeanour, the specific accoutrements in which they manifest – are, to the best of Sunny's knowledge, predominantly a matter of personal taste and preference. She's never entirely understood, therefore, why so many of them *choose* to look as they do: to appear before the still-alive in rattling chains or caked in filth, with missing heads and absent limbs, bloody daggers protruding from their chests or gaping wounds across their throats.

Or, in Godiva's case: naked, and on horseback, a visual reproduction of a folk legend likely no more representative of Godiva in life than a green felt hat and longbow were of any of the medieval Robin Hoods.

Would not a tailored gown and brooch pin better suit a Lady?

"I can't say that I do," she admits.

"It is that I might remember." Godiva draws the blade free of its fastening and examines its edges. "Remember Leofric and tend the flame of my wrath. You are familiar, of course, with the story of the parade – the uncloth'd shame brought down upon me, then and always, by that ferret-eater and his balladeers?"

Sunny rakes over the thin leaves of what new knowledge she's accumulated lately around this particular local legend. Leofric, the tale goes, was prone to raising taxes – so high, and so often, as to impoverish the people of the kingdom over which he ruled. Godiva, soft of heart, implored her husband time and again to show mercy, to free his subjects from the shackles of this poverty, and time and again Leofric refused. Until, at last, he relented – on condition that the beautiful Godiva ride naked through the streets to Cofa's Tree, as proof of her commitment to the cause.

How much do you really *care for them, Godgifu? How far are you prepared to go?*

A peculiar way to demonstrate one's decency, no doubt. But Sunny has lived and occasionally waded through the organised indecorum of enough stripped insurrectionists, from the Bashorun Gaa dissenters to the SlutWalkers of Toronto, to recognise the value of a naked protest.

"I know *of* the story," Sunny says. "Though I confess some ignorance of the shame you mention. I was under the impression you *chose* to ride the streets, unclothed?"

"*Chose* it?" Godiva's roar turns the night-time air to cinders; would scorch the grass, had the archaeologists allowed any to remain around the gravesites. "You believe, daemon, that I would *choose* to bare myself before God and all His servants?"

"No?"

"No!" Godiva breathes deeply of the heated air – through habit alone, Sunny has to assume. "I know something of this land, this present tense," she says, more calmly. "I hear the voices of my supplicants, imploring me. I hear the living, chittering like blackbirds all around me in a hundred foreign tongues. I have even heard," she smiles at Sunny, "some snippets of your Aretha Franklin and your Cell Block Tango. I am not so ignorant as you fancy of the customs of the day, of its colloquia. And I *know*, daemon, how its people speak of me. The tales they tell. But they are wrong.

"The parade, Leofric's *horse ride*... It was never a protest. Never some private spat between man and wife spun out into public spectacle. It was punishment. Another penalty to pay for my *unwomanly* insubordination. It was not the first nor the worst of his inflictions, but he might just as well have slung me naked in the stocks or had me pilloried as had me bared and exhibited for all the townsfolk to behold. By God's bones, the humiliation would have been no less."

"I see," says Sunny, and indeed she does. She herself has met a thousand men like Leofric, a thousand wives like Godiva; a *thousand* thousand. Men who delight in the abasement of the women they believe their property. Who revel in their suffering: the indignities doled out in the open, and the torments inflicted behind closed doors.

Men like Anand Kumar and Dean Weller. Women like Natasha Larkin and Kiran Nagra.

Small wonder Godiva turned an ear to that child's prayers.

"You are thinking," Godiva says, observing Sunny's changing expressions, "that the men I hunt for my petitioners are *not* Leofric. That I will not be cleansed of him through their disposal."

Again, Sunny shrugs, entirely noncommittal. Better, she suspects, not to second-guess the Lady, nor to underestimate her apprehension of this secular modernity and its *profiling* techniques. Perhaps Godiva too has encountered *Criminal Minds* and the novels of Thomas Harris; perhaps she, like Sunny, is aware that any catharsis achieved through the extermination of surrogates will only ever be short-lived, and that no destruction, present or future, will grant her lasting satisfaction.

Really, what Godiva *ought* to do is seek out Leofric, or whatever remains of him, and take her vengeance upon *him*, and not this recent shower of proxies – however repugnant each was in life.

"Actually, what I was *thinking*," Sunny begins, the beginnings of a plan coagulating to concretion as she speaks, "is that it's a shame you *didn't* kill Leofric while you could. It might have saved us all a lot of trouble. You might then have had no need of these other boys you've been dispatching – Weller and Foy and so on. Indeed, were Leofric to appear before you *now*, and were you to do to him as you have to *them*... I daresay you might find yourself stepping back from slaying altogether. Giving yourself a holiday from the slaughter, as it were. A little rest."

Godiva considers this. "Perhaps. But what of it, daemon? Leofric is gone. Rotted and fed to the soil a millennium ago, and I have no means of resurrecting him so that I might take my justice. *I* am no necromancer. I cannot raise the dead to gratify my whims."

"True," Sunny says – and hopes, as she positions herself towards her final gambit, that she'll have *something* of value to offer Jonas in exchange for the very large favour she'll soon enough be asking of him. "But in fact, I know a man who can..."

CHAPTER 16

SUNNY

"All's well that ends well, then," Bunny says, scooping sesame seeds from a sticky rib with an oyster fork and popping them into her mouth. "Assuming Godiva is as good as her word?"

Sunny forces down another bite of her xiaolongbao. Observes but refrains from commenting on the chalk-like pastry of the wrapping and the under-seasoned pork within. "She will," she replies, on swallowing. "There may well be *other* murders soon enough in the vicinity of Cofa's Tree – we can only do so much, can we not? But they won't be at Godiva's hand. She is... well, let's say she's *at peace now*, shall we?"

This is, of course, a lie. Godiva's peace, though promised, has not yet been paid for. Jonas must still work what magic he can, and is willing to, on the spirit of Leofric, wherever *he* might be. Before *that*, moreover, Sunny must induce the boy to do so.

There's been, she reflects, altogether too much persuasion required of her lately.

"How wonderful." Bunny gnaws happily at the

remainder of the rib. "And you'll be returning to London shortly? By air, I imagine. Though I'd be delighted to call for a car, if you'd prefer."

"Still eager to get rid of me, I see."

Bunny pouts. "Obviously you must stay as long as you wish. *Obviously.*"

"Oh, do stop *fussing*, Berenice." Sunny swills a mouthful of Tieguanyin tea about her palate and, finding it satisfactory, relents a little. "I shall be off this afternoon. By means as yet undetermined. Rest assured, however: you shall not be inconvenienced. The Midgrove Shakespeareans shall lose not a moment of their Olivia."

Bunny relaxes into her overstuffed chair, her concerns ameliorated.

"There is, however, just one more thing," Sunny adds – gratified to have, at last, the opportunity to wheel out the phrase.

"Oh?" Bunny tenses anew.

"You recall my telling you the girl Kiran attributed her knowledge of the magicks to the TikTok?" She stumbles, deliberately, over the syllables of the last word, its rogue definite article placed entirely by design. It will not do to give away too much of her newly acquired digital proficiency; not yet.

"Yes?" Bunny answers, distractedly. "A terrible worry, that such things can be found on the internet. I really must look into it."

Sunny considers the ageing desktop computer gathering dust in the study along the hall: the most visible possible signifier of a creature for whom contemporary technologies hold neither interest nor allure.

"And yet," she says, "when I myself went searching for this... online sorceress, I found nothing. Which is strange, is it not? One would think a practitioner so powerful as to bewitch a young girl through the intermediary of a screen would leave *some* trace of that power. Some... aftertaste."

"I'm afraid it isn't my area." Bunny rises from her throne and begins to clear the dishes from the table.

"Nor mine, Bunny. Nor mine. But I found it unusual, nonetheless. And since, as you say, it behoves us to understand such things, I... *did some digging*. Paid, in fact, a follow-up visit to the girl Kiran. The thrall cast over her is strong – I saw as much myself, at Godiva's graveside. But I asked myself: might not there be alternate means of eliciting some further clue or other from the girl, as to the identity of our unknown sorceress – our UnSor, if you will? Some less direct method of questioning, through which one might... *work around* our UnSor's enchantments to happen upon the necessary evidence?"

Bunny pauses in her drudgery, hovering stock-still over the table, stained dishes piled in her hand.

"Do you know, therefore, what I did, Bunny?" Sunny continues – so calm, so *amiable* she might have been commenting on the weather or an item on the local news. "I simply *talked* to the girl. No thrall, no compulsion on my part. Just... friendly chat. Probed her for what I thought might prove useful context. For yet more embedded clues to chase about thereafter like a bloodhound. And I'm pleased to say, she was happy to indulge me." She grabs for the teacup before Bunny can swipe it away, drawing out the moment with two long, leisurely mouthfuls of the Tieguanyin. "You know, I think she may just have been eager for someone to talk to. About her life, and her interests. Her... hobbies."

Below the stack of crockery, Bunny's hand begins to

shake. Imperceptible to the human eye, perhaps. But not to Sunny's.

"I realise, on reflection, that I ought to have considered the possibility sooner. That I ought not to have taken everything I learned at face-value. And in fact – and you must believe I was *kicking myself* later for having forgotten – she *did* mention at the Priory that she'd dabbled in theatre, as a student." Sunny takes a sip of the tea, savouring its sweetness. "Though *you*, of course, know that already, do you not, Bunny? I daresay she might have alluded to it, when she joined your troupe of play-ers. Certainly, she must have when she was crowned Viola to your Olivia. So many scenes for the two of you to tread together on the boards. So many moments of intimacy you must have shared in those *many*, many rehearsals you've enjoyed."

"I don't...," Bunny starts, but neglects to finish. "I'm not..."

Sunny takes pity on her. Extends a crooked finger to the empty chair. "Sit, Bunny. Sit, and let me tell you how I believe this bloody saga to have unfolded. Exposition is the detective's hallmark, is it not? Moreover, if I may: you seem apt to choke on your own tongue if you continue, so it may be better for us both for you simply to listen while I speak."

Bunny's mouth closes and grows taut, as if tightened by invisible screws. She hesitates, briefly, then lays down the plates, and sinks wordlessly into the chair.

"Here," Sunny says, the commingled spirits of Holmes and Columbo, Benoit Blanc and Peter Wimsey working through her, "is what *I* believe to have happened.

"Let us return, if we may, to an evening two months or more before the *now*. It is a Monday, 6 or 7pm, and you, Bunny, are already installed – as is your fashion – in the rehearsal area of the Midgrove Shakespeare Society: no doubt some draught-ridden parish hall leased at an exorbitant rate from the Anglicans or the Methodists. You are early, eager to slip into character, and thus you are alone, keenly awaiting the arrival of your co-stars, your director. Until - lo! Who should push through those grey fire doors but your Viola, Kiran! You rise to greet her, perhaps to offer her a biscuit... and you observe her distress. Her terrible, terrible distress.

"You ask her: *what's wrong? What could possibly have caused her such upset?* And she, reeling from the thing that has traumatised her – or perhaps simply trusting you, a friend who is nevertheless at one at a remove from her immediate circle – allows something of the tale to flow out from her, albeit in fragments. Briefly, you learn of the man from her office who has wrought some grievous but thus far unspecified injury upon her; of the messages she has just that day encountered, exchanged over telephone between this man and other, brutish beings like him. You learn of the girl's terror, and her rage.

"You beg her for specifics, so you might begin to present to her some practical solution. To *help* her, as is your wont. But, alas – you are interrupted, the arrival of some other of the Midgrove players throwing the girl into a mournful silence in which she remains for the entirety of the evening's rehearsal, the recitation of her own lines notwithstanding.

"This cannot do – this *will not* do. Not for you, Bunny. No human grief shall go unexpurgated on *your* watch. So it is that, when the rehearsing is done – the coffee cups rinsed in the communal kitchen and the polypropylene furniture stacked away – you seek her out anew, the girl. Perhaps you walk with her to her bus-stop, or drive her home in that jalopy of yours. The earlier conversation continues. And through her unburdening, you learn the details of Dean

Weller's crimes, and of the roles carried out by his accomplices.

"You think fast; you must, for soon the girl will be gone. It may be a week or more before you see her again. You're aware, as are we all, that no *direct* action can be taken on your part: *you* cannot rend these human monsters limb from limb, however appetising the prospect. But a great wrong has been done here, and *someone* must act. And then it hits you: there is a spirit in your very midst, in the *girl's* very midst, who may be better placed to take this vengeance for her. I assume *you* were aware of Godiva and her penchant for a righteous kill prior to that evening. Might you even have... greased the wheels of some of them, before?

"Perhaps? We'll never know.

"In any event: Godiva, you realise, it must be. Quickly, you put into motion your plan, hastily assembled though it is. You thrall the girl; implant in her the knowledge of the grimoire and how she might use it – *where* she might use it – and, most importantly, *to what end*. Though I must wonder, given how alarmed she was on seeing what became of Jonathan Foy and the others, just how *much* you revealed to her of Godiva's modus operandi.

"And thus, your work is very nearly done, with just a few loose ends to tie up thereafter – not least the physical conveyance of the grimoire itself to the girl. Did you deliver it in person to her residence upon retrieving it from your collection, or was a courier service employed to do your bidding? We must hope, if the latter, that they handled it with care.

"But wait!" Sunny feels her inner Poirot take the wheel, steering her to her denouement. "Even as you prepare to free her from the thrall, you realise: the girl *cannot be allowed to remember* it was you who gifted her this knowledge! In planting the suggestion, you have, in the current vernacular, *taken a shit where you eat*. And the girl, whom you see and *will be seeing* so frequently, cannot know you as anyone but kind, maternal but fundamentally ineffectual Am-Dram Bunny: unrivalled as a shoulder to cry on, but as practical in a crisis as a chocolate teapot. You require a cover story. A *red herring*, that might convince even the girl herself that she has happened upon the plan – and *the means by which to execute the plan* – elsewhere. And so is birthed the saga – the *entirely confabulated saga* – of the TikTok witches and their necromantic prowess."

Bunny opens her mouth, the better to issue outraged denials, forcing Sunny to silence her with a raise of the palm. "I know what you will say here, Bunny. Computers are *not your area* – how, therefore, could you possibly have known to leave such a trail of neologistic breadcrumbs? And it may be that they are not – that the computer in the study is indeed your sole connection with the virtual and the digital. But do you not read the papers? Do you not keep abreast of current affairs on the News At Ten? I put it to you, Bunny, that you do. And that, whether through a *Panorama* special or a featured article in the Guardian, you've learned more of the idiosyncratic crevices of the internet than any might suspect on looking at you. More than enough to fool the unconscious of a trusting human. To fool *me*, to my shame."

Her case rested, Sunny reaches again for her tea.

"You know," Bunny says, "we're always looking for new members, at Midgrove. You might consider coming along, with that flair you have for the dramatic."

"Am I wrong, Bunny? Have I misrepresented your conduct, in the telling?"

For a moment, Bunny is still. Thoughtful. Then: "Surely

you, of all people, don't judge me for... whatever I may or may not have done? You, who've cared not a whit in the whole of your existence for the suffering of others?"

Again, Sunny shrugs. It's a reasonable point, certainly. Although she wonders, now, how truly accurate the statement is, since the events of the last year or more. Since Jonas; since Miranda.

Might it be that even *she* is capable of change? Of – and she shudders even at the phrase – *personal growth*?

"What now, then?" Bunny adds. "Now you've worked out for yourself what happened here – what you *believe* to have happened here. What now?"

Sunny regards Bunny: her ringlets and her apple-cheeks, her simmering indignation and her burning sense of justice. One not so terribly different, in the end, from Godiva's. Or from Miranda's, come to that.

"Now," she says, "I go home, as we discussed. But perhaps we might have dinner sometime, just the two of us? My treat."

AUTHOR'S NOTE

I've played fast and loose with the specifics of the Godiva legend, and the Lady herself, here. My apologies therefore to scholars of Old and Middle English, and of 11th century European history.

All mistakes and inaccuracies are entirely my own.

Effusive thanks, conversely, to the greats of detective fiction that inspired this story: Agatha Christie, Walter Mosley, Raymond Chandler, Val McDermid, Dorothy L. Sayers, Marion Chesney, and a hundred more besides.

Thanks, likewise, to the characters who inspired Sunny in her dogged pursuit of (a kind of) justice: Hercule Poirot, Jane Marple, Agatha Raisin, Benoit Blanc, Easy Rawlins, Lieutenant Columbo, Detectives Olivia Benson and Elliott Stabler, Philip Marlowe, Jessica Fletcher and Agent Clarice Starling, among others.

Neither she nor I could have done it without you.

AFTERWORD

Thank you so much for reading.

Reviews mean the world to indie authors like me - so if you've enjoyed this story, I'd love it if you'd take the time to visit Goodreads or Amazon and tell other readers how you feel.

All the best,
    T.C.

ABOUT T. C. PARKER

TC Parker is a writer and researcher based in Leicestershire, not too far from Coventry, where she lives with her partner and family.

The author of the El Gardener crime trilogy (*The Debt, The Push* and *The Remembrance*, recently reissued as *The Long Con* omnibus) and the horror novels *Saltblood, A Press of Feathers, Salvation Spring* and *Hummingbird*, she's been a copywriter, a lecturer and, very briefly, an academic. Now she runs a semiotics and cultural insight agency by day and dreams up stories at night, when the kids are asleep.

Visit her online at www.tcparkerwrites.com, and subscribe to her newsletter at tcparker.substack.com

ALSO BY T. C. PARKER

Horror & SF/F

Saltblood
    Salvation Spring
    Hummingbird
    A Press of Feathers
    Maiden (with Ward Nerdlo)

Crime & Thriller

The Long Con: An El Gardener Omnibus
    The Debt
    The Push
    The Remembrance

Romcom

Taking Flight: A Sapphic Screwball Comedy

HUMMINGBIRD

There's a storm brewing in Gallow: angry parents, protests at the school, a new priest up at the church with some very clear ideas on sin... and an unfamiliar face in the cottage on the edges of the village, carving sculptures out of skin and bone.

It's a powder keg. Even before the protestors start disappearing...

Buy It Now On Amazon

Jodie doesn't want trouble - just to be left alone to raise her son in peace.

Tanya wants more God and less wickedness in her own son's studies.

Tara wants to leave her complicated past behind her, if only it would let her go.

And all Jonas wants is to get some work done - and if he can make peace with his father while he's at it, then so much the better.

But the woman in the cottage and the priest up at the church - they have very different goals in mind. And Jodie and Tanya, Tara and Jonas... they're about to get caught in the crossfire.

With a Foreword by Stephanie Ellis, author of Paused *and* The Five Turns of the Wheel

SALTBLOOD

**A remote island. A group of prisoners.
And an evil as old as time.**

Robin didn't mean to break the law. Didn't
know at first what law she'd broken. And
now she's on her way to Salt Rock - a new-
model prison for a new kind of criminal,
way out in the remote Northern Isles of
Scotland.

Buy It Now On Amazon

On Salt Rock, she'll meet other prisoners
like her - men and women from all over the world, spirited away
from the lives they knew for crimes they didn't know they were
committing.

She'll uncover the complex web of conspiracy that connects them
all, confronting some of the darkness of her own past in the
process.

And she'll come face to face, finally, with an evil as old as the land
itself.

It's hell in those waters.

A PRESS OF FEATHERS

Anger... it can eat you alive.

Rage.

Bea has it - more than ever, since her husband left her. Lou has it - has it in spades, since she lost her job and her flat and had to move back in with her parents.

Buy It Now On Amazon

And whoever's been murdering and mutilating the men whose bodies keep mounting up in Bea and Lou's city - they've got it, too.

But when Bea moves to The Gates, an exclusive new estate with a strange and troubled history, and Lou's interest in the murders leads her right to Bea's door, the two women find the lines between nightmare and reality, history and myth and sanity and madness blurring around them - and a primeval entity born from the chaos of creation with her own appetite for rage rising up to meet them from the ground below.

She sees them. And she's hungry.